Take One Step

WILLIAM E HALLEWELL

TAKE ONE STEP

Take One Step
© 2025 by Will Hallewell. All rights reserved.

No part of this book may be reproduced, stored in a retrieval system, or transmitted in any form or by any means - electronic, mechanical, photocopying, recording, or otherwise - without prior written permission from the author.

This is a work of fiction. Names, characters, businesses, places, events, and incidents are either the products of the author's imagination or used fictitiously. Any resemblance to actual persons, living or dead, or actual events is purely coincidental.

ISBN: 979-8-9934717-3-0 - Paperback Edition
ISBN: 979-8-9934717-4-7 - Electronic Edition
ISBN: 979-8-9934717-5-4 - Hardback Edition

Cover design by Will Phillips Hallewell
Published by Phillips and Dunn Publishing

Author's Note:

This book contains scenes that portray suicide through symbolic images and metaphors. I want to speak directly to you before you read further, because these moments are not meant to describe what actually happens to a soul after death. They are mythic, emotional landscapes, not statements of doctrine, theology, or - especially - judgment.

I do not believe that those who struggle with despair, mental illness, or suicide are lost or condemned. I believe in a God whose grace reaches farther than our darkest moments, a God who meets us in our pain, and a God who restores what has been broken. Nothing in this story is meant to diminish that hope.

The scenes you will encounter - forests, shadows, thinning places, worlds that shake apart - are metaphors for the inner battles we face, the despair that can trap us, and the love that reaches into the hardest places to pull us back toward life. They symbolize the emotional realities many of us carry, often quietly, sometimes for years.

In truth, this story became something deeply personal as I wrote it. It started benign, just a seed of an idea, but then it helped me face parts of my own past I had never fully dealt with. It helped me grieve my father in ways I didn't know I needed, and it helped me recognize the depth of the love I have for my wife, Hollie: the kind of love that saves, restores, and holds on even when the world feels thin. And believe me when I tell you, she dragged me a long way down the metaphorical tracks toward freedom from my demons.

This book is fiction, but the emotions behind it are real.

That being said, if you have ever struggled with despair or lost someone you love (haven't we all?), I hope you find in these pages not a picture of hopelessness, but of rescue. Not punishment, but redemption. Not final darkness, but a light that reaches deeper than grief.

And if you or someone you love has suffered through thoughts of self-harm, let this be said clearly: you are not alone. You are NEVER alone. You are loved. Grace is real. And there is always hope.

If you ever feel lost, overwhelmed, or in danger of harming yourself, please reach out. You can contact the Suicide & Crisis Lifeline by dialing 988 in the United States, or speak with a trusted friend, counselor, or pastor. Help is real, and you deserve to receive it.

Thank you for allowing me to share this story with you. It came from a place of pain, healing, memory, and love, and I offer it with a full heart.

— *Will*

For my Mom, my Dad, and my family.
You are my rock.

Dedicated to:
My amazing wife, Hollie
30 more years, baby.
I love you – always.

PREFACE:

There are moments in life when the world feels thinner than it should be; when time hesitates, when memories seem so realistic that they press against the edges of reality, and when the love felt in those memories becomes the only thing strong enough to hold us steady.

Most of us never speak of these moments. We may tilt our heads, we may wonder silently or in secret with someone who won't judge us, but it is these memories that shape our lives and give *us* purpose. We all stand on the traits of those we have loved and who have gone on before us.

Every family has a story born from such places - a story of someone loved, someone lost, someone holding on a little too tightly, or letting go far sooner than they ever wanted.

This story came from one of those thin places.

It began with a simple question: What happens to a soul caught between the life they lived, the life they longed for, and the life they never had the chance to see? And what does love look like in a world that doesn't play by the rules?

For Tim, Laura, and Rose, their journey is not simply about trains or shadows or strange places between worlds. It's about grief that reshapes us. It's about the fierce, unbreakable pull of family.

It's about the kind of love that steps into the darkness and refuses to turn back. It's about the courage to never give up or give in – to warrior up when things get hard - really, really hard.

If you've ever felt the world grow fragile beneath your feet, if you've ever loved someone so deeply that the thought of losing them rearranged your very heartbeat, if you've grieved, hoped, doubted, prayed - then you already know the language of this story.

So listen closely.

Pay attention to the rails beneath your feet and the whistle that echoes from far-off places.

The journey begins simply enough.

A step.

A breath.

A crossing of worlds.

All aboard.

Part One

All Aboard

PROLOGUE

A Cow and Family

A black and white spotted Jersey cow stood eye to eye with Tim as he stood there in the field, the heavy mist of the morning dropping wet dew on the grass. The weeds and sparse clumps of wildflowers sagged beneath the weight of that dampness, their colors muted, as though still waking up. Breath flowed from the cow's broad nostrils in steady bursts, each one unraveling into a pale mist like that of a cold winter's day. A lone tree stood to his right, its bark darkened by moisture, while to the left lay a small crest of hills that he often referred to as mountains when he was much smaller - back when things were better.

Tim briefly questioned why there was mist when it wasn't that cold outside; the thought passing like a curious cloud across his mind. He tested the air with a deliberate breath through his mouth and shrugged when his vapor matched that of the cow's.

Somewhere beyond the animal, the countryside stretched into a soft gray fade. Smaller trees dotted the distance, and the fence from which the cow had apparently escaped leaned in defeat. A section once whole now lay broken, and he wondered if the animal had pushed its way through with purpose or simply wandered into freedom.

It struck him, absurdly, that his last act on earth might be exchanging breath with a cow; human and bovine vapors mingling invisibly in the damp air.

From the trees, a bird broke the silence, singing to greet the slow-blooming sunrise. Tim answered with a whistle, the sound a faint ribbon in the mist, then lowered his gaze so his eyes locked with the cow's. The animal didn't flinch. It simply stared back, its own dark eyes unblinking.

"Don't judge me, please," Tim murmured, turning to look east where the sun's first colors brushed the sky. As he spoke, he realized these words might well be his last.

"I'm talking to a cow. Perfect." The bird replied with a cheerful trill. "What a great way to end an existence." He sighed. "It was a feeble existence, but an existence nonetheless." He took in a breath thick with the scent of wet earth, let it out in a long exhale, and offered the bird a sad smile along with another whistle.

Tim looked again toward the broken fence, then back at the cow, tilting his head slightly as if posing a question. "Are you lost, my friend, or did you decide to venture out on your own, or..." He paused, scanning the empty landscape; no farmhouse, no barn, just the skeletal line of fence. "...or are you just here for the show?"

The cow bent to tear a mouthful of grass and lifted its head to chew, the motion slow and deliberate. A rope of saliva swung and fell to the trampled clump below. Tim scrunched his face, chuckling softly. "Just here for the show, then, I guess. Well," he glanced back at the ruminating creature, "that's fine if you want to watch. When it happens, however, don't judge me."

Turning again to the east, he sighed, his breath heavy with meaning. He used to love the sunrise with its fantastic palette of deep reds, purples, and blues, splashed with molten yellows and oranges. Clouds then had seemed soft, harmless, bringing with the dawn the promise of hope. Back then, morning felt like a gift. Now the rising sun only reminded him that time was relentless, unmoved by anything humans did. "It's as if we don't really matter after all," he said to the cow, who answered only with a puff of vapor from his nostrils. "Eh, what do you care?"

Then came the sound, faint at first, then swelling, the whistle of a train approaching a curve to his left, cutting through the valley and ricocheting off the mist-covered hills like a battle cry. Tim closed his eyes and saw a plume of white steam curling up from a black smokestack, the locomotive roaring with grandeur through this very field. Somewhere deep inside, reality whispered that such engines had been replaced by the dull hum of diesel, but his mind refused to yield.

He was safe in that memory: *kneeling beside his father as their model train rounded the bend from under a papier-mâché mountain they'd built together. The tiny smokestack puffed with simulated smoke, and his father's smile radiated pride. From the record player, Sinatra's My Way drifted in, softened by the gentle hiss and pop of vinyl. "There's no one better than Frank," his dad had declared before nodding toward him. "Hit the whistle."*

Seven-year-old Tim had pressed the button, sending out a tinny sound that, to him, was as real as any full-sized train. That remembered whistle merged now with the one in the present, both swelling into a single call. He opened his eyes and turned toward it.

Every nerve in his body sparked alive. His hands trembled. A tear broke loose, followed by another. He stepped closer to the tracks, leaving the cow behind both physically and mentally. His eyes closed once more, and in his mind, he was again the boy from decades ago, looking up into his father's face.

"How do I do this, Dad?"

His father's brow furrowed. "What's that, son?"

"How do I do *this*?"

The diesel engine rounded the bend, its single headlight burning into him like an unblinking eye. Peace rose in him as he felt - no remembered - his father's hand on his shoulder. "Just take one step, son. Whenever you're afraid, when you don't know if you can go on, take one step and see where it leads. Then take another, and another."

"I love you, Dad."

"I love you too, son."

And as the train bore down, Timothy Wentz took that step. The bird sang one last note, and the cow, with dignified finality, bid him farewell with a low "Moo."

"Clack–clack, clack–clack, clack–clack..." The ritualistic rhythm of the train wheels beneath him told Tim something wasn't right. He had stepped *onto* the train, not *in front of* it.

He opened his eyes slowly, letting them adjust to the dim interior of a passenger car long past its prime, its most vital commodity, passengers, absent. Shadows pooled and shifted with the sway of the car. Rows of seats stood in faded silence, some split at the seams, stuffing peeking through like old wounds - others bearing small, dark holes. The upholstery's colors were dulled to near guesswork in the gloom, though age had clearly worked its way into every thread. A faint, dry scent of aged fabric mixed with the sharp tang of machine oil and the heavier aroma of warm grease from the engine just ahead. The combination wrapped around him like the ghost of a memory.

He turned toward the window. Beyond the glass, there was nothing. There was darkness so thick it seemed to press back against the pane, a tangible black that could almost be touched. "I should be..." his voice trailed into the still air as unease tightened in his chest. He rose carefully, the motion swaying with the train's momentum. "Exactly where is this? Am I dead?" His voice cracked slightly. "And, if this is... death, then where exactly does this train go?"

A breeze, impossible yet undeniable, slipped through the car, cool against his cheek, whispering past his ears. It curled around him, insinuating itself into the space between skin and bone. His breath caught; his throat constricted, each inhalation narrower than the last until it ceased entirely. Reflex took over, his hands clawed at his throat, then pressed against his chest. His knees buckled, and he dropped back into the seat with a thud that echoed in the hollowness of the car.

"Dad?" The thought barely formed before a familiar weight settled on his shoulder, strong and steady, the same as before, out there in the mist, with the rising sun and the cow's silent judgment.

"Don't judge me," he had told the cow. And then, his father's voice cut through...

"I see you took the step, Tim. Way to be brave." The voice was close, warm, but Tim's head shook in panic. "Dad, I can't breathe."

His vision narrowed, the edges clouding. The shadows deepened, pooling in the corners until they seemed to seep in through the windows themselves, swallowing the car whole. The train's swaying slowed, but the iron wheels still chanted their "clack–clack," even as the sound began to stretch and fade, like something heard underwater.

Then the blackness tore apart.

A flood of light, blinding - golden, burst through, enveloping him in heat as much as brilliance. Instantly, the car's details sharpened: the alternating red and blue seatbacks, the far wall's paint curling in tired strips, the conduit lines jagged in places where the casing had broken. Overhead, the mismatched pattern of grimy ceiling tiles and glass panes admitted the blaze of day.

Tim turned to the window on his left and gasped.

Under a sky of impossible blue, rose a hillside dressed in lush, carefully kept grass. Deep beds of violets lined the slope, so rich in purple that he could almost smell their heady, lavender fragrance through the glass. Daisies punctuated the violet with bright white petals and sun-yellow centers. The hill's green ribbon of grass curved upward to the right, vanishing behind a small stand of trees. Through the branches peeked faint white blossoms, lilies, perhaps - though his thoughts had no time to settle on the question.

A group of people rounded the bend, heading toward the train.

At first, they were vague shapes, no more than silhouettes. Then, as if some switch inside him flipped from wonder to recognition, the faces cleared. His family. His mother and father, his aunts and uncles, and his grandparents, all smiling as they approached.

And there, Uncle Max. Boisterous, irrepressible Uncle Max, his curls a genetic match to Tim's own. He lifted a hand in a sweeping wave. "Hey, Timmy! How the hell are you? C'mon. Come with us, it'll be good to have you with us after all this time!"

Max had been everything Tim's father was not: loud, reckless, full of wild ideas and bets that sometimes paid in laughter - sometimes in blood. That recklessness had eventually caught up to him, brutally. A street corner, a flash of violence in the brutal form of a gun, life spilling away before the eyes of his family. The memory was a bruise that never healed, and Tim could still see how it hollowed his father.

Life wasn't supposed to work that way.

But sometimes it did.

Uncle Max's image brightened as if stepping into a spotlight, but Tim's lungs pulled tight again. Once more, he gripped his throat, gasping. Around him, the train seemed to pick up speed. Shadows grew denser at the edges of his vision.

More family crested the hill, voices calling his name, hands reaching as he struggled for air. His grandmother, in her ever-present dress, and his grandfather with the kind eyes, and the warm, embracing hug. They all came to greet him, and he supposed that was the way that place worked. All loving, all love.

Aunts, uncles, and cousins all moved toward him with open arms, and his vision became dimmer. The waves of relatives slowed, and suddenly, his mother was beside him. His head lolled to the side and landed on her shoulder. So kind, so gentle.

She smiled and extended her hand. Tim took it, the familiar warmth and softness wrapping around him in an instant. Her scent filled him; gentle soap, faint perfume, something entirely *her*, saturating him from skin to marrow. The flood of memory and longing left him momentarily incapable of forming a single thought.

He had missed her love. Her kindness. Her beauty. He had missed it all. But she, too, had been claimed by the ghosts of that cursed house. Another summer day, another innocence stolen in the span of a breath.

The darkness snapped away and was replaced.

"Stop sign!" His younger self screamed the words as his mother's car sped toward an intersection, the red octagon ignored, the oncoming box truck barreling through on the cross street that had no stop sign. The basketball rolled from his hands as he tore down the pavement, as if sheer will could intercept her. "Mom! Stop sign!" The cry echoed off neighborhood houses, useless against the inevitable.

"I know, dear," she said now, her voice calm as her breath swept gently over him. The terror of that day ebbed from him in slow retreat. Her smile glowed faintly as she whispered, "I'm sorry."

He wanted to tell her he forgave her. He wanted to tell her he loved her. He wanted to say everything at once, but instead, he gasped hard, pulling in air as though surfacing from deep water. He was slowly able to breathe again. His family faded, climbing back over the hill, their hands raised in a soft, collective goodbye. And then... they were gone.

Tim lifted his own hand toward them, but the train jolted with a metallic thud as the brakes shrieked, pulling him forward into the seat ahead. His head struck the backrest, a blunt knock that sent him sprawling to the floor.

It took seconds, long seconds, for his lungs to fill fully again. Rubbing the back of his neck, he eased himself upright. The darkness outside the windows had been replaced by warm light spilling over a station platform.

The place looked as though it were pulled from another era: wooden canopy glowing under soft yellow lamps, black wrought-iron fence tracing the edge of the platform, neat gravel beyond. Benches stood empty, their slats worn smooth by years. A brick building with inviting rows of windows stood at the center, its doorway framed beneath a sign that read only *Café*. There was no hint of a town name. No timetable. Just that one word.

Tim stayed seated, caught in the quiet nostalgia of the scene. No one boarded. No one departed. His hand absently massaged his neck, the air sweet and easy in his lungs now.

Then his father's voice crackled through some hidden speaker, breaking the stillness. "This is your stop, Tim. Time to unload." A click followed, and the café's interior light bloomed like a silent summons.

Tim stood reluctantly, stepping toward the door that now yawned open. "Is this... heaven, Dad?" The shadows of the car offered no answer. "Am I going with..." He gave a glance over his left shoulder toward the window and the once green hills that were now replaced by darkness.

At the threshold, he paused. The scent of steam and grease rose from the idling locomotive, mingling with the soft warmth of the evening air. The memory of mist and a cow's breath brushed the edge of his mind, and he smiled at the symmetry of it. "If this is heaven," he mustered a joke in deference to his father, "I hope they serve decaf. Last thing I need is eternal jitters."

Off to his left, white smoke curled into the night from the locomotive's chimney. He thought of his father again.

With no idea where he was or what lay ahead, Tim smiled, said, "Moo," and stepped off the train. He didn't know the destination, but he knew, finally, that he was ready for it.

CHAPTER 1

The Beanery Queen (or Lack Thereof)

The small bell above the café door jingled as Tim stepped inside, its delicate chime trailing a few moments after the door had closed. He turned back to glance at it, a tiny gold bell suspended on a black bracket, still quivering from its motion. Simple, unassuming, effective. The kind of thing that, years ago, might have kept his fascination for minutes at a time. *It's just a bell on a bracket on a door,* he mused. Yet here it was, doing its job flawlessly. Even... here. Wherever this was.

The air was touched with the tang of freshly mopped floors, a faint lemon cleaner scent riding on the warmth of the room. Rows of wooden barstools lined the counter, their cracked black vinyl cushions worn from years of use. Empty cherrywood tables waited like soldiers at attention, condiment racks at their centers standing guard.

On the far wall, a large painting of an old steam locomotive pushed forward into a snowstorm, black smoke curling against the pale blizzard. Just above eye level, a miniature train ran an endless circuit along a narrow track, wheels humming quietly with each pass.

Somewhere deeper in the café, Frank Sinatra's *Fly Me to the Moon* swirled around him, a familiar voice carried on gentle static from an old speaker. Nostalgia settled over him like a warm coat. *There's no one better than Frank,* he thought, scanning the café for a hostess; half-expecting, half-knowing this wasn't that kind of place.

He chuckled under his breath. "This is a beanery, not a café," he muttered. Years of his father's train obsession had dragged him deep into railway lingo. At one point, he'd even made a list: beanery, the café hogger, the engineer, the boomer, the nomadic worker - but somewhere along the line it had vanished, likely swallowed up in the wake of his father's passing.

"Hey, where's the Beanery Queen?" he called into the open space, his voice light with humor, clearly not expecting any reply.

"There isn't one," came a softness that caught him so off guard that he spun on his toes to face the person who had uttered the words. His breath caught.

She sat alone in a corner booth, a beautiful woman with sandy-blonde hair that might once have curled loosely but now hung limp, as if defeated by long hours of neglect. Her lips formed a rigid, indifferent line; her eyes, a soft, rich brown, carried a weight of sadness that seemed carved into her very being.

Tim's smile softened, coaxing warmth into the space between the two of them. He stepped toward her. "No Beanery Queen? Then who's supposed to wait on us?"

"It's self-serve," she said, lifting a mug from the table, tone flat.

He glanced toward the counter and the gleaming stainless steel coffee station behind it; spotless carafes, glass pots resting on warmers, the faint hiss of heating elements working.

"Help yourself," she said, the words carrying the weight of *go to hell* as easily as they did an invitation.

Tim chose to take them at face value. He moved across the room and poured a cup, breathing in the rich aroma before even tasting it. Somehow, even the coffee's scent tugged at the thread of his father's memory. But when he turned back toward her, the woman's expression pulled him away from that warmth and back into the present as if an invitation to let go.

"There's cream and sugar on the table next to the coffee," she added, eyes still down. "Might be sandwiches in the fridge."

"Sandwiches?" He crossed to a silver refrigerator and opened it. Rows of neatly wrapped sandwiches, slices of pie under glass domes, vegetables in crisp containers, all lined up as if awaiting an unseen shift change. He chose a slice of apple pie and returned to the booth.

"Just like America - coffee and apple pie." He held them up with a grin.

Her eyes lifted just enough to meet his. She cupped her mug as though trying to draw some secret warmth from it, and offered a subtle nod.

"Not so sure about the coffee," she murmured, the faintest smirk tugging at her lips. "Okay, to the pie. But America? Not so wholesome anymore."

He slid into the seat across from her. "Pardon me?"

She sighed, responding to his silent, *mind if I join you?* "Apple pie's supposed to mean wholesomeness - like America used to be. But America isn't that fu..." She stopped, eyes dropping again.

Tim pulled out the chair across from the woman and sat. That's when he saw the scars - thin, pale lines along her wrist, the kind that spoke of sharp edges and quiet desperation. He looked away quickly, but not quickly enough.

"Lines on my face, you know?" Her voice was quiet, flat.

"I never asked."

"Yeah, well, you looked. Same thing."

His ears burned from the verbal stabbing. "I apologize. I didn't mean to upset you."

She waved the words away. "Happens all the time. At least here."

He took a bite of the pie, letting the sweetness fill the awkward space. "That's damn good pie."

"They do have good pie here," she said without much inflection. "Whoever makes it knows what they're doing."

"Best coffee, too." He sipped, savoring the deep roast. "Hell of a beanery."

Her eyes lifted again, still sad, but curious now. "Are you just here to critique food?"

"Well... if the afterlife has Yelp, I want to leave a good review." He waited, but she didn't react. So, he chuckled at his own joke.

"Not exactly sure why I'm here. But I am. So... I'll just have to deal with it."

An odd stillness settled between them.

Finally, he extended a hand. "Tim Wentz."

"Laura," she said, the corner of her mouth lifting ever so slightly. "Laura Palmer."

She took his hand and the handshake lingered a heartbeat longer than necessary, a quiet connection neither wanted to name.

Tim smiled at Laura, feeling that same current pass through their joined hands a second time. "Pleasure meeting you here, Laura. Even if I don't know where *here* is."

"You're at the café." Her tone was matter-of-fact as she opened her arms in an encompassing gesture, but the tiny glint of humor in her eyes was the first light he'd seen there.

He grinned. "Got me there. Beanery, technically. Proper railroad lingo."

That coaxed a real smile from her, brief but disarming. They sat in companionable silence for a time, sipping coffee, the quiet hum of the model train overhead marking the moments.

Tim set down his cup. "Do you have family around here?"

Her expression shifted, the humor gone as quickly as it had come. "Here?" She gave a small, dry chuckle before glancing toward the window and the softly glowing platform outside. "I did, briefly. But they're not around anymore. They certainly aren't *here*."

A flicker of recognition lit Tim's eyes, and he offered an educated guess. "Did they come from over that hill? Your relatives?"

Her head tilted, a hint of curiosity replacing her guarded detachment, her eyes briefly lighting up with hope. "So you've been there, too?"

"I'm not exactly sure where *there* is. But on my way here, I saw a lot of my relatives." He leaned forward, lowering his voice like a conspirator. "Dead relatives."

Laura's mouth twitched, but her tone stayed flat. "Happens all the time on the train. People see them. Then they stop here for coffee and act like I'm supposed to have the answers. I'm not a caretaker. I'm just... here." She gestured to the café around them. "Like you."

His brow knit, the words settling over him like a cold draft. "You mean I'm..."

"What, you haven't figured it out yet?" Her smirk was tinged with something between amusement and pity.

"No," he admitted, glancing around as though the walls might explain themselves.

"This place..." she began, voice lowering. "It's neither here nor there."

The air between them thickened. Even Sinatra seemed to have faded as if Frank himself were listening; the only sound was the soft hum of the coffee station.

"I don't know how to take that," Tim murmured, gripping his mug in both of his trembling hands.

"You don't know how to take the fact that you're not dead? Or that you're stuck in... limbo? In-between?"

Tim gave an awkward glance away. "Well... It's not usually the kind of news you get before coffee."

She leaned forward, eyes suddenly sharp. "All joking aside, let me ask you something. How did you get on the train, Tim? You think it just stopped by your house and a conductor shouted, 'All aboard'?"

He dropped his gaze to the coffee, avoiding her stare. The image of the cow in the field flashed in his mind. The whistle. The step.

Laura slid her wrists forward, pale scars catching the light. "This was my ticket. Thought I'd paid the price. Then... I woke up on that train. I've been stuck here for two days, waiting for answers. I suppose back there I'm still... lying in that tub..." She paused. "Now and then," Laura whispered, "I'd hear something...

muffled noises, like someone calling my name, but far away. I thought I was losing it."

Tim's voice was almost a whisper. "I stepped in front of it. The train. I guess that was my ticket."

"Well, aren't you the brave one?" she said, though her sarcasm carried less bite than before.

The words brought back his father's voice: *Way to be brave, Tim.* It sent a shiver down his spine.

He cleared his throat, desperate to move on. "Have you been beyond the café? *Is there a beyond?*"

"I'm not sure." She turned to the window again. "I've tried stepping out, but... nothing. I can see the platform, the lights, the mist, even trains passing. But once I step outside... it's gone. Like a mirage. I follow people, hoping I can stay in their wake, but it's all... nostalgia for me. Just a painting I can look at, not touch."

Tim chuckled softly. "Coffee, pie, and contemplation."

"Dire contemplation," she corrected with a small smile.

He stood, drawn toward the front door. He crossed to it and his hand found the cool metal of the handle.

"You can try it," she said, her voice suddenly softer, nodding toward the door. "Maybe it'll work for you. But..." She hesitated, still gazing out the window.

"But what?"

She looked at him, and for the first time, the sadness in her eyes came with something else... fear. "You're the first person here I've wanted to talk to. When we shook hands... I felt it. A connection. I don't want you to go. If you leave, I think I'll be stuck here again. Alone."

Tim's lips curved and his eyes spoke his excitement. "Good. So it wasn't just me."

A whistle cut through the air - deep, commanding. Both turned toward the door, then cast their gazes toward the window.

From somewhere outside, a voice called: "All aboard!"

"Dad?" they said in unison, different voices in their minds, but the same summons.

Tim met her gaze, a smile forming on his lips as if he had made the paternal connection. "I think it's your time, Laura. Time to board. Are you coming?" He pushed the door open, holding out his hand. "I'll go if you go. Let's see what this limbo has to offer."

She hesitated, eyes darting to the safety of her cup.

"Come on," he urged. "If you can't, I promise I'll stay. We'll figure it out together. Adventure awaits."

Her lips curved into the faintest smile. "What the hell?" She slid out of the booth. "Maybe this time I *can* escape. Maybe it's meant to be."

At the doorway, she took his hand. They stepped together into the warm night air, the platform solid beneath their feet, steam curling from the great black locomotive before them.

"You're still here," he said, joy in his voice.

"I know." Laura let out a huge sigh of relief. "Let's get the hell out of here before someone changes their mind."

They climbed aboard side by side, their steps in sync. Whatever this in-between world was, they were going to face it together.

CHAPTER 2

Holding Hands with Susie Moreno

If someone had asked Tim at that moment whether it felt strange holding Laura's hand as they boarded the train, he would have said yes. Though who was there to ask him? His father? That was impossible. His dad had been gone for years, along with most of his family. Tim supposed that was why he was here in the first place: too many empty chairs at family dinners, too many losses too soon. The grief had curdled into depression, and the depression had eventually carried him to his own end. Here... in limbo.

It was hard to start a relationship when you were drowning inside. Most people didn't want to carry that weight for someone else. So no, there was no one to ask him now, not even his father, though Tim could have sworn he'd heard his dad's voice on the train before – but not now. Not when he needed him.

That didn't make the question any less important. This was the here and now. And there *was* something about Laura, something that had sparked between them back in the beanery. So the question remained: did it feel strange holding her hand? Truth be told, Tim hadn't held many women's hands in his life, so no, it didn't feel strange at all. It felt... nice.

The first girl's hand he'd ever held belonged to Susie Moreno, way back in the sixth grade. The memory curled a smile onto his lips. Laura noticed as she sat down on the cracked leather bench two-thirds of the way back in the train car, its springs groaning under her weight. The front of the car was swallowed in shadow.

"What's the smile for?" she asked, sliding over to make room.

Tim crossed the aisle, easing down beside her. The leather gave a tired sigh beneath him. "Just thinking about the first time I held a girl's hand." He gave her hand a light squeeze.

"Oh?" Laura teased, tilting her head and smiling at him. "And what was her name?"

"Susie Moreno." His voice carried the same kind of pride other men reserved for talking about touchdowns or first cars. Truthfully, he hadn't thought of Susie in years. "All the way back in sixth grade."

Without fanfare, the door to the train car slammed shut on its own. A heavy clunk echoed through the car as the brake released, and the train began to roll forward. The slow, steady gathering of speed made Tim close his eyes for a moment, feeling the familiar sway and low rumble beneath his feet. It reminded him of the model train his father had built, paper-mâché mountains and all.

When he opened his eyes again, he smiled at Laura. The empty car didn't bother him anymore; the absence of porters, ticket takers, and engineers had simply become part of the odd logic of this place.

"And what about you?" he asked. "Who was the first boy lucky enough to hold *your* hand?"

Laura's eyes flicked upward in thought, and her palm drifted to the ceiling above them. The glass roof, meant to frame sweeping mountain views, showed only darkness. "That would have been fifth grade. Davy Jones. And no, not the singer or the pirate. Just a geeky boy with braces and a slide rule." She gave a soft laugh. "I wish he'd been the singer. Maybe things would've turned out differently." Her wrists turned upward for a moment, the scars catching the dim light. "Or not. I don't know. I try not to play *what if*. It's too painful. Doesn't change anything anyway."

Tim nodded in understanding. "And whatever happened to this Davy Jones of yours? Doctor? Lawyer? Computer programmer?"

She stared straight ahead into the shadowed seats. "I'm... not sure. His family moved away in seventh grade. I never saw him after that. We lost touch."

"You could've looked him up on Facebook," Tim suggested. "I've done that with some old friends. Never found Susie, though..."

He stopped mid-thought. A faint light had begun to form up ahead, spilling weakly over a side-facing bench near the front of the car.

Laura, still talking, didn't notice at first. "That would've been nice..."

Tim held up a hand to quiet her, his gaze fixed. "Do you see that?"

Her head turned. "What is it?"

"I'm not sure..." His voice trailed into a whisper. He rose, the train's sway forcing him to grip the overhead rail. Laura's hand slipped from his, falling back into her lap. "Oh my God."

In the pale light sat a woman so thin she looked carved from bone, arms wrapped tight around herself despite her hoodie and jacket.

Laura called Tim's name, but he didn't answer. Some deep recognition stirred inside him, and his pace quickened. When he reached the woman, he laid a gentle hand on her shoulder.

"I know it's been forever," he said softly, his concern so deep it shattered even him. "But... are you Susie Moreno?"

Her head turned slowly, as though her joints were rusted. Hollow eyes studied him. "I'm sorry," she rasped. "Do I know you? Do you know where I am?"

"Tim. Tim Wentz. Sixth grade... we were friends. You... held my hand once."

Something flickered in her gaze. He smiled faintly. "How have you..." But he caught himself. Here, he quickly realized, people didn't arrive by accident. Lowering his voice, he said, "I'm sorry. I shouldn't have asked."

"It's okay, Timmy," she said, using his old nickname. "I had breast cancer. I couldn't take the panic, the anxiety. So... here I am. On the..."

"The suicide train," he said quietly, putting one and one and one together as their voices blended in the darkness.

She looked around at the gloom. "I guess. Before this, I was in a forest. Black trees, everywhere. I felt as if I had become one of the trees. I couldn't find a way out. It was so dark... and there were things in there. Biting." Her voice trembled. "I was there a long time. Then I felt..." She smiled in recognition and held a skinny hand to Tim's face. "I felt... you. Like I was back in sixth grade... holding your hand. The darkness lifted, and I was here."

Tim took her hand in both of his, sitting beside her. He gestured to the back of the train. "Laura and I think this is some kind of limbo. Between heaven and hell. We're just riding to see where it goes."

She leaned close, her whisper sharp, her eyes darting. "If there's hell for people like us, Timmy, that forest is it. Don't send me back, Tim. Please."

When her sobs came, he wrapped her in his arms. "I don't know how to make sure... but I can hold you, Susie. If you want."

She fell into his embrace and clung to him with a tightness reserved for a rescuer. Warmth flowed - not *from* him, but *through* him. Slowly, her shivering stilled. Color returned to her cheeks. Her frame filled out beneath the hoodie. Her smile grew, radiant and whole.

"I don't know what you're doing to me," she murmured. "But don't let go." She pulled in closer.

"I won't," Tim promised.

When at last she pulled back, her eyes were bright and she looked almost... alive. "So this is what it feels like to be close to Timmy Wentz, huh?"

He chuckled. "Guess you should've held my hand more often in sixth grade. Actually... it was all downhill from there, so you probably made out."

They sat quietly until the train's brakes hissed and sunlight poured through the glass above. Susie stood, kissed his forehead, and glanced toward Laura with a grateful wave.

"Thank you for coming, Timmy. I'm free to go now."

The doors slid open, revealing a world of green hills, wildflowers, and golden light. Without looking back, she stepped into it.

When the doors closed again, Tim returned to his seat. The light faded. Laura took his hand, resting her head on his shoulder. "That was sweet of you."

"I'm not sure what I did," he admitted, "but I'm glad I did it. I hope she finds peace."

"I hope we do, too," Laura murmured, already drifting into sleep.

Tim smiled as the whistle called and the train rocked them onward, the clack of the rails like a lullaby.

CHAPTER 3

I nterlopers

The mighty train rambled on in the darkness, its travel unimpeded, as Tim and Laura slept soundly. Their heads rocked gently with the car's motion, their breathing slow and even. Outside, the night was a pitch so complete the engine itself seemed to vanish into it, no moon or stars to give it shape.

Inside the stillness, something changed.

It wasn't colder. It was warmer - a dry, breathless heat like the air when an oven door opens. A faint metallic tang of iron and singed paper threaded through the aisle. Overhead, the lamps gave a soft, apologetic flicker, as if a shadow had moved behind their power. The glow steadied. The train hummed on.

Along the murky route, somewhere deep in the darkness, a figure appeared in the car.

His entrance was not the slow rise of a ghost or the stomp of a regular passenger. One moment, the aisle was empty; the next a man stood there, as if he'd stepped out of the fabric of time and into night itself.

He could have made any romance-novel lead rethink his trade. Properly pressed blue jeans, a white V-neck island shirt open enough to show thick tufts of chest hair, and black oxfords with brown trim. Shoulder-length salt-and-pepper hair swept back from a strong brow, a face both rugged and refined; somehow, he was both middle-aged and young at once, made more striking by the steady confidence he wore.

He saw Tim and Laura sleeping in the rear of the train car and cocked his head, a sly smile revealing perfect white teeth. His eyebrows lowered, weighing some private question.

"Well, well," he said softly, voice smooth as dark liquor with a whisper of heat beneath. "Interlopers on my train."

The word wasn't tossed off. It carried weight, a curious edge. Not disdain for stowaways, but interest in a problem.

He walked back toward them, unhurried. As he moved, his palm tapped each seatback, slap, step, slap, step - a ritual he seemed to enjoy. He stopped by their row and regarded them in silence. His eyes lingered a heartbeat too long on their joined hands. Something in his expression flickered, equal parts amusement and calculation.

"You two don't belong here," he murmured, almost to himself, as if testing the shape of the thought. Then he straightened. "We, however, will have to have our visit later, I'm afraid... interlopers. I'm a bit busy right now."

He turned gracefully, shirttails wafting, and took his place at the front of the car. Hands folded in front of him, posture loose, he let the train's rhythm rock him.

Confused, frightened, sometimes reluctant passengers began to appear, as if drawn from the very molecules of the dark. Some clutched themselves. Some stared wide-eyed. None knew quite how they'd arrived.

He went to each one in turn, his voice dropping to a private whisper, as if the question was for them and them alone. "Are you certain?" The question barely stirred the air. A nod. A flinch. A slow, resigned yes. With a flick of the back of his hand, they vanished, gone as neatly as they'd come. Most struggled to meet his gaze; those who did looked away quickly, as if heat lived behind his eyes.

When the last passenger was dispatched, he glanced back at the sleeping pair. He stepped close enough that the dry warmth pressed faintly against their skin.

"You two are... different," he said, studying them as though trying to find a connection to something tangible. "I'll deal with you later. For now, adieu. Enjoy your ride."

Then, he was simply gone. The metallic scent thinned. The lamps brightened to their usual hum. The train rolled on.

Tim and Laura slept on, unaware.

After a couple of hours of hypnotic traveling had passed, the brakes squealed, and the train slowed to a complete stop. Sunshine flooded the car from the windows above as the door slid open.

The change in motion woke Tim the way a car's deceleration nudges a dozing passenger. He blinked, took in his surroundings, then touched Laura's shoulder. She stirred, eyes finding his, and he pointed toward the open doorway.

"I think this is our stop," he said, nodding again for emphasis.

Beyond the door, the light was honest and warm, a welcome contrast to the gloom that had colored everything since his arrival in this in-between. The air moved into the carriage in lazy curls, warm and salt-tinged, and trailed across their faces.

"Wow," he breathed. "Wherever we are, it sure feels nice. Better than anything I've felt in a very long time."

"Do you really think this stop is for us?" Laura rubbed sleep from her eyes, her voice a shade more cautious than his. She didn't share his certainty, not yet.

"Well, there's only one way to find out." Tim stood and took her hand. "Let's go. If we can't get off the train, then I'm pretty sure it isn't our stop. I felt it when Susie left. There was no way I was making it out that door, so I didn't even try. This, however, feels different, so let's do it. We won't know unless we take that one step." He held up a solitary finger on his right hand.

"Is that some kind of crazy pep talk?" Laura stretched, a small smile tugging at her mouth. "That take-one-step thing. Is it supposed to motivate me?"

Tim chuckled, a touch embarrassed. "It's just something my father used to say. When I hesitated on a big decision, he'd tell me, 'You know what you want to do. Now take one step. The rest will be easy. Take that step and see where it leads. See what road you go down.'"

Laura raised an eyebrow. "Did that work?"

Tim shrugged. "It worked on me... well, sometimes. Other times Dad had to bribe me with pie."

"Well," she said, standing suddenly and tightening her grip on his hand, "let's take that step together, you and I, and see where it leads us. And, just for the record, just in case, I like pie."

They walked hand in hand to the doorway and looked out.

A huge ocean stretched before them, blue sky reflected in long rolling sheets of water just beyond a pale ribbon of sand. The heat of midday rose in soft waves, carrying the steady hush of breakers folding themselves along the shore. They drew in slow breaths, looked at one another with growing affection, and took that one step.

Together.

CHAPTER 4

New Beginnings

The unexpected couple stepped down from the train and onto warm sand, blinking in the sudden burst of sunlight. The air shimmered with heat, and the fine grains shifted under their weight, each step sinking slightly before springing them upward again. They were midway between the boardwalk and the waterline when, almost in unison, they turned back. The train was gone - not a trace, no lingering whistle, no faint rumble. Just the open expanse of beach stretching endlessly in both directions.

"Hmm," Tim muttered, shading his eyes and scanning the horizon where the rails should have been. "Now what? Our ride's gone without us."

"I'm not sure," Laura replied, her tone far more casual than his. She tipped her head back, closing her eyes to the blazing sun, and lifted both arms to the sky as though greeting an old friend. "But if this is where we have to stay for the rest of our... existence, I'm down with that. I wasn't exactly a fan of that train anyway."

"Great," Tim flapped his arms in playful resignation. "I didn't bring sunscreen. If I start glowing, tell me it's something otherworldly and not sunburn."

The breeze caught strands of her hair, carrying with it the briny tang of the ocean. She inhaled deeply, a soft smile breaking across her face. "I love the beach. It's always brought me peace. I should've gone to the beach more often instead of... brooding over my life. Things might have been different." Her voice faltered slightly on that last part, but before Tim could reply, she seized his hand and took off running. "Come on, let's see what we can find!"

"I don't even know where we are!" Tim called after her, stumbling a little but laughing despite himself. The sudden burst of playfulness felt alien and yet exhilarating.

"Who cares?" she shouted over her shoulder, pulling harder. The sun painted her hair gold as she barreled toward the water, a joy that had been suppressed for so long, now spreading across her lips.

Tim gave in, letting the rhythm of their sprint strip away the heaviness he'd been carrying. Each pounding step seemed to drive the weight deeper into the sand until it was gone entirely.

They didn't slow at the water's edge, however. Fully clothed, they plunged in, the surf exploding around their legs, the first shock of cold stealing Tim's breath before the rhythm of the waves took over. The salt clung instantly to their skin, the wind teasing the wet fabric against them. Laura brushed her hair back from her eyes, then launched a volley of splashes at him with gleeful abandon.

"Hey, no fair!" Tim sputtered between laughs, storming toward her, legs cutting through the water's resistance. His splashes grew more aggressive, sending arcs of cold spray into the sunlit air until she raised her arms to shield herself, laughter still bubbling from her chest. "You're lucky I failed swim team," he spoke with playful enthusiasm. "I would have been dangerous."

When he finally reached her, he caught her in his arms, more to stop the assault than anything else. The motion stilled. They stood there, breath slowing, waves nudging against them, eyes locked. There was no need to speak, but Laura did anyway, her voice soft, almost reverent.

"So... it's not just on the train," she said, gazing up at him. Her expression softened in a way he hadn't yet seen.

"I'm not sure what you mean," he murmured.

"That feeling. The ease. Remember what I told you before we boarded? I still feel it. Here. With you. As if..."

"As if it were meant to be this way," Tim finished for her. His voice was steady, but something inside him trembled.

"Exactly," she breathed. "As if it were meant to be this way."

For a moment, the space between them seemed to narrow of its own accord. Tim felt the urge to lean in, to close that last fraction, but he held himself back. The restraint burned, but yesterday, if it was even "yesterday" here, they'd both stood on the edge of ending everything. Maybe this was too much too soon.

He let her go gently, catching the subtle dip of her gaze, the brief flicker of disappointment. "Are you hungry?" he asked instead.

She followed him toward the shallows, her voice quieter now but tinged with something hopeful. "Sure. As long as it's not cold cuts from some ghostly café in limbo."

"Beanery," he corrected with a grin, trying to lighten the moment. "Let's see what we can find."

Soaked through and dripping trails of seawater behind them, they trudged away from the surf. The sand clung stubbornly to their clothes and skin, each step releasing small bursts of heat from the sunbaked surface beneath. As they walked, the glare of the sun forced them to squint and shade their eyes.

The beach around them was alive with a mosaic of strangers; bright umbrellas flapping in the breeze, towels patterned in loud tropical prints, sandcastles already succumbing to the incoming tide. Boys and girls darted in and out of the waves, while couples strolled the shoreline, their laughter swallowed by the roar of the ocean.

Tim's gaze wandered to a few men whose sunburned bellies shone like overripe tomatoes, their swim trunks riding dangerously low. "Man boobs," he muttered under his breath, grinning.

Laura caught his look and flushed, realizing she'd been caught silently judging a group of older women in mismatched bikinis, their neon hair catching the sun. **She looked away, embarrassed, then leaned over and whispered, "It's like a highlighter exploded."**

Tim snorted. "Chartreuse is a cry for help." He waved his hands in a mock plea.

She covered her mouth, laughing harder now, and shook her head. "We're terrible."

"Absolutely," he said, still smiling. "But at least we're united in our awfulness."

"People are crazy," she said, slipping her hand into his.

Overhead, the sudden shriek of military jets ripped the air apart. Both of them looked up instinctively, following the metallic shapes slicing through the blue, the noise ricocheting off the hotels lining the boardwalk. A tour helicopter traced slow circles beyond the breakers, its shadow skimming the water below.

They passed rows of umbrellas and sand-covered towels until the weight of wet socks grinding against gritty sand became unbearable. Tim stopped. "Hold on. My feet feel like they've been fitted with cement blocks." He crouched down, unlacing his shoes.

Laura followed suit, her hair falling forward as she worked at a stubborn knot. Tim's eyes lingered, not on the sunbathers all around, but on her. Her beauty. Somehow, in the middle of all this bright chaos, she was the only one in his frame.

She glanced up. "Strange, isn't it? We've still got the same clothes we had on when... well, you know."

Tim slid off his socks, grimacing at the clumps of wet sand sticking to his hands. He patted his pockets and pulled out his wallet, still intact. "Huh. Wallet's here. Keys too. Guess everything transfers with us. Good thing, otherwise, lunch would've been a challenge."

Laura dug into her own pockets and pulled out a wad of damp bills, holding them up so droplets fell into the sand. "I never carry a purse. But I usually carry my money. Such as it is." She smiled, and the momentary cloud from the beanery was gone.

Tim laughed, comparing her dripping bills to his slightly drier stash. "Let's use mine for now. Yours can sunbathe later."

She tucked the money away, picked up her shoes, and grinned. "So... this is a proper date then? The man buys?"

"That's right," he said, taking her hand.

Her smile faded slightly. "I'm not sure I've ever had that before."

"Well, you do now."

Tim started to glance at her, but the sand was scorching his bare feet and diverted his attention in a hurry. "Yeow! We'd better move before my soles melt off."

They took off running, the heat nipping at their heels. Halfway to the boardwalk, Laura's foot caught on a hidden ridge, and she went down, hands and knees sinking into the sand. She burst out laughing.

Tim dropped to help her up, but she seized his arm and yanked him down with her.

Before he could react, she straddled him, leaning down to kiss him hard, ignoring his brief hesitation until he gave in. The salt on her lips mingled with the taste of the ocean air. Above them, a black parasail drifted across the sky, emblazoned with a skull and crossbones. Tim's breath hitched, an uninvited omen, but he closed his eyes and let himself sink into the warmth of her.

When the kiss broke, Laura rocked back onto her knees, brushing sand from her hands and tossing back her hair. His cheeks were flushed. "I was going to do that back in the water," he admitted, "but I wasn't sure..."

"Yeah, I noticed." Her tone carried a mock sternness as she stood, pulling him up. "Don't do that again. Be confident. Take the step. This..." she gestured to everything around them "... is rare. Maybe this is a second chance. We don't have time to waste."

Tim smiled, leaned in, and kissed her again, softer this time.

From here on, he thought, that step would be easier.

After the second kiss, they brushed themselves off and ran the remaining stretch to the boardwalk, the coarse grit on their skin itching with each step. Laura wrinkled her nose at her sand-caked hands. "I'm a mess. Let's hit that rinse station before I start exfoliating myself raw."

The rinse station stood like a small oasis, water hissing down over the concrete. They took turns stepping in, the cool spray washing the clingy sand from their feet. Laura's eyes scanned the other beachgoers, some chatting in groups, some sprawled in the sun, others heading toward the bars and arcades.

"Do you think they can tell?" she asked suddenly.

"Tell what?" Tim replied, rinsing his calves.

"That we're... you know... partially dead?"

Tim grinned at her phrasing. "So that's the official term? Hello, I'm Tim. I'm partially dead."

Laura laughed, switching feet under the spray. She raised her eyes to him questioningly, "Got something better?"

"Somewhat dead? Not really dead? Dead to a degree?"

She pretended to ring a game-show bell. "Winner, winner! Dead to a degree."

He chuckled, then looked out over the crowd. "You don't suppose everyone here is, uh... like us?"

She shrugged. "Maybe. Maybe they're all bad actors in a celestial play, but this..." she squeezed his hand "...is *our* meant-to-be. Let the rest figure out their own path."

When they were finished rinsing, Tim offered her one of his socks as a towel. She made a face, and he laughed, stuffing it back into his shoe. "Alright, air-dry it is. We'll find a store. Socks can't be that hard to come by."

Hand in hand, they wandered a short way down the boardwalk before stopping at a towering bronze statue of Neptune. The sea god loomed above them, muscles taut, one hand gripping a trident, the other resting on a turtle, with an octopus curling below.

Tim smiled faintly, his memories flooding in. "Virginia Beach," he spoke, the memory flooding back. "I used to come here with my parents. Dad loved it. He'd sit right on this boardwalk, watching the ocean while Mom ran. I remember when they put this statue up. I must've been thirteen or fourteen." He wiped quickly at a tear. "Feels like another life." His voice softened on the last words, his gaze lingering on Neptune's weathered face.

Laura traced the statue's lines with her eyes. "I always wanted to come here. Never got the chance. Life has a way of… getting in the way."

"Well," Tim said, slipping his arm around her shoulders, "you're here now. Together with me. Let's make the most of it."

Her stomach growled audibly, breaking the moment. She laughed. "Agreed. But can we do it while eating?"

He offered his arm gallantly, and she took it. Barefoot, shoes in hand, they left Neptune Park and crossed into the strip.

The street was a riot of storefronts and signage, souvenir shops crammed with beach towels, t-shirts, sunglasses, trinkets, and even live hermit crabs in tiny painted shells. Every few steps, a new scent drifted from the open doorways: fried dough, coconut sunscreen, fresh pizza. Somewhere behind it all, the ocean's briny tang still lingered.

They ducked into a shop where Tim grabbed a pair of socks and a towel. Outside, they sat on a bench to dry their feet before pulling on their shoes.

"Apparently, wet money spends just fine," Laura said as they stood.

"Probably happens all the time. We are at a beach," Tim replied. "As long as we've got dry feet again, I'm happy."

"Then let's eat," she said, smiling up at him.

They wandered toward 19th Street, following the hum of the crowd and the scent of garlic drifting from a small Italian bistro tucked between a surf shop and a boutique. Its soft, golden light spilled onto the sidewalk, a welcome contrast to the fluorescent glare of the souvenir stores.

"This place looks perfect," Laura said, eyeing the menu in the window. "I could go for real food. Homemade food."

Tim held the door for her. "After the beanery, I'm ready for anything."

Inside, the air was cool and faintly scented with basil and baked bread. A single guitarist strummed quietly near the back, the notes mingling with the clink of glasses and the soft murmur of diners.

"This is cute," Laura whispered as Tim pulled out her chair.

"I just hope they serve people who are dead to a degree," he teased.

Laura's eyes widened for a second, then she laughed. "I never thought about that."

A young waitress with dark hair in a ponytail approached. "Welcome to Nineteenth Street Italian Bistro. My name's Alisa. I'll be your server. Can I start you off with something to drink?"

Tim put on a serious face. "Do you serve people who are dead to a degree?"

Alisa blinked, then grinned. "We serve everyone. Believe me, I've seen it all in five years here."

"Great," Tim said. "In that case, let's order."

Laura chose a Chipotle chicken wrap with fries; Tim debated between vegetable stromboli and meat-and-cheese ravioli before opting for the latter. When Alisa left, their eyes found each other across the table.

"I've never had this before," Laura said softly, taking his hand gently in hers.

Tim frowned. "Had what?"

"Being treated like this. Doors opened. Chairs pulled out. Your dad must've taught you well."

Tim's gaze turned inward, his voice almost nostalgic. "He did. He treated my mom like she was royalty. *Sweetheart*, this - *darling*, that. They were... madly in love. After she died..."

Laura looked at him, surprised. "Oh. I didn't know. I'm sorry."

Tim's voice trailed off slightly before he added, "Yeah, she ran a stop sign and got hit by a car that didn't have to stop. I was playing basketball up the street. I yelled for her, but... of course, she couldn't hear me."

Laura squeezed his hand. "It sounds like there was nothing you could've done."

Tim nodded slowly, but a shadow passed over his face. "I know, but my dad never recovered. He drank. Got mean. My brother ran away, leaving me to deal with the wreckage. I've never forgiven him for that." He looked down at his lap, but never let go of Laura's hand and the security it brought him. "Eventually, Dad's drinking killed him. After that..." Tim's voice caught. "I got bitter. Depressed. Started using things harder than alcohol. And that... led to the rope. He shook his head, a bit of confusion running through his mind. No, I mean the train." His eyes flicked up to hers.

Laura gave his hand another squeeze. "I'm sorry to pry. One thing at a time."

Just then, their salads arrived. The waitress grinned. "Two salads for a couple of people dead on their feet."

"Dead to a degree," Laura corrected, smiling.

Alisa laughed. "Right, my mistake."

They ate quietly for a moment before Laura spoke again. "My turn." She wiped her mouth with her napkin, swallowed her food, and looked at Tim as if she were confessing. "I was abused, one way or another, most of my life. Foster homes. Some bad. Some worse. I don't need to embellish what's going through your mind. It's all true. My sister and I bounced from place to place, never fitting in, never feeling safe. People either hurt us or ignored us until we were moved again. That kind of thing... it stays with you." Her voice was becoming more and more intense, and when she finished, she looked away and brushed tears from her face.

Tim started to ask her if that was how she got her scars, but she waved the question off and courageously moved along as if she had been explaining the wounds for years instead of days. "Not yet.

One thing at a time." She offered up her best smile, and the subject dropped without any protest from Tim – just a knowing nod.

They finished their meals, paid with their damp bills, and stepped back outside into a sky brushed with deep purples and golds.

Moving the conversation past the awkward ending at the restaurant, Tim glanced at the horizon and the lowering of the sun. "Guess we know how late it is."

Laura's stomach gave a playful growl, and she chuckled. "Ice cream?"

"With your wet money," he said.

She grinned. "Sounds like a plan."

The ice cream shop was wedged between a kite store and a neon-lit arcade, its sweet, creamy scent wafting onto the boardwalk. Laura slapped her wet bills onto the counter with a grin, ignoring the young employee's mild grimace as if she'd just handed him seaweed. Tim chuckled under his breath. "I don't know about him, but I'll have Oreo," she said, giving a backward nod toward her date.

Tim smiled and said, "Ditto," placing his hand on Laura's back.

Cones in hand, they stepped back into the warm evening. The sun sagged lower in the west, gilding the boardwalk in bronze light, the ocean beyond glowing like molten glass. Their ice cream began to melt faster than they could keep up, dripping over fingers and down the sides of the cones.

"Race you," Laura said, taking a big bite.

They both laughed as they devoured what they could before the cones collapsed completely, the sweet cream mixing with the taste of salt in the air. Somewhere along the way, they agreed it must still be summer; the warmth, the crowds, the tang of sunscreen and fried food hanging in the breeze all whispered it.

Atlantic Avenue pulsed with life. Shops spilled their wares onto sidewalks, racks of T-shirts printed with mermaids and sharks, bins of sand pails and plastic shovels, strands of fake pearls catching the lamplight. A pair of shop employees smoked out front, barely glancing up as a group of tourists browsed the display tables, and the smell of colitas rose through the air in a silent tribute to the Eagles. Both Tim and Laura scrunched their faces and stepped away from the nauseating smell.

A tour bus lumbered past in the slow lane, its diesel breath hanging in the air, competing with the marijuana. Tandem bikes rolled by, chains clicking, the riders awkwardly in sync. Pedal cars trundled forward, the drivers laughing at the surprising effort it took to keep them moving, and the nuisance of teenagers on electric scooters added to the chaos.

They passed a booth where teenage girls, too young for real tattoos, got intricate henna patterns drawn on their hands and ankles. The girls giggled at the daring of it while their parents watched with an odd mix of resignation and disapproval.

Further along, the brightness of the storefronts gave way to shadows where buskers strummed guitars for change. Some had talent, others simply had a hat to catch coins. Then there were the ones who had neither... only a hollow stare and an empty cup.

Against the brick wall of a closed shop was a cluster of three huddled in sleeping bags, their backpacks close as lifelines. Their eyes, dulled by fatigue or hunger or both, barely tracked the movement of the boardwalk.

A man with stringy, graying hair reached out and caught Tim's wrist. His voice rasped, damaged from years of cigarettes or something darker. "Spare change?"

Tim patted his pockets, finding nothing. "No, sorry, man." He moved to step away, but the man's eyes lifted to meet his. In that moment, Tim felt the contact like a cold hand against the back of his neck.

If he didn't know better, he would have sworn the man could see *through* him, deep enough to touch the truth of what he was... and why he was here.

The man's lips twitched. "God save you, son." Then his gaze broke away, almost as if disturbed by what he'd found.

A faint warmth flared under Tim's skin, the same metallic taste brushing his tongue that he'd felt back on the train. He pulled Laura along quickly, eager to escape the man's stare.

When they'd gone far enough, Tim forced a lighter tone. "I don't think I could go that far. Living on the streets, I mean."

Laura glanced back toward the cluster of the homeless, and she shrugged gently. "*They* haven't tried to board the train yet. Maybe they still have some hope left."

Tim nodded, but his thoughts were still tangled around the man's eyes, the strange echo of recognition in them.

Nearly six blocks from where they'd stepped onto the sand earlier, music began to weave through the crowd; warm, soulful notes carried on the salt air. Tim's head turned, a smile already tugging at his lips.

"Do you like to dance?" he asked.

Laura tilted her head. "Depends on the music."

He grinned. "Sounds like Motown to me."

They followed the sound to where the boardwalk opened onto a small park. A stage had been set up against the backdrop of the ocean, the surf's low roar blending with the music. A banner read *BJ Griffin and the Galaxy Groove*. The cellist-turned-frontman swayed as he sang, the band spilling out a mix of Motown and classic rock that felt like it could hold the night in place forever.

Tim took Laura's hand, and without hesitation, they began to dance barefoot at the boardwalk's edge. Their new socks had turned damp from their wet shoes that now slung in their free hands, and they let the rhythm carry them. Others joined in, a ring of strangers drawn together by the beat, the laughter, and the ocean breeze.

For the next hour, they forgot everything. The train. The questions. Even the ache of their pasts. There was only the sway of their bodies and the music curling around them.

Somewhere behind the crowd, a shadow leaned against the railing, too still to be just another onlooker. The lamplight caught its profile for the briefest instant, then it was gone, slipping into the folds of the night.

Laura never saw it. Tim thought maybe he had, maybe a few brief locks of blonde, but the band hit a high note, and she pulled him into a spin, her laughter shaking the thought from his mind.

When the final chord faded, the crowd cheered, and BJ Griffin's voice rolled out a warm goodbye. Laura, cheeks flushed, tugged Tim's hand. "Come on. I'm tired. Let's get something to drink."

He made a show of pouting but let her lead him away from the music. "Fine. But I'm counting on the train not showing up just yet."

Laura smirked. "Then you'd better drink fast."

They crossed Atlantic Avenue, slipping into a narrow bar lit in low amber. A few locals hunched at the counter, the hum of a muted TV blending with the clink of glassware. Tim and Laura found a small table near the window, the salt-warped wood cool beneath their forearms.

They ordered without fuss, beer for him, something bright and fizzy for her, and for a while their talk skimmed over safe, surface things. The band. The boardwalk. The way ice cream in summer somehow always dripped faster than you could eat it.

But then Laura's gaze slid to the street outside, to a man curled in a doorway across the way, a shopping cart of battered belongings beside him. She stirred her drink slowly, the ice shifting against the glass.

"How do you think people let themselves get so low?" she asked quietly. "To end up living on the streets like that? Not just here. Anywhere."

Tim's answer came quicker than he expected, like it had been sitting just under his tongue all night. "I don't know. How do people let themselves get so low that they board the train we boarded?"

She looked at him but didn't speak, and for a long, uncomfortable moment, there was silence.

He shrugged, eyes on his beer, then finally broke that silence. "Sometimes life just... wears you down. You stop asking for help. And people stop offering, even if they see you drowning. After a while, they don't want to be bothered. Too awkward. Too heavy. So, you either disappear into the streets... or disappear completely."

Her hand found his across the table, warm and steady. "Then I'm glad I caught the right train," she said, squeezing gently. "Glad it was the one that brought me here. To you."

Tim swallowed against the lump in his throat. "Me too."

Somewhere in the corner of his vision, in the dim reflection of the window, there was movement again - this time a tall, blonde figure leaning in the shadows of the far wall, too far inside to be waiting for a table, too still to be just another customer. For half a second, Tim thought he saw a faint curl of a smile before the man vanished, as if he had simply blinked out of existence.

He blinked, too. And when he looked again, there was nothing but the dusty outline of a framed picture on the wall.

He didn't mention it.

They left the bar and stepped into the warm night, the boardwalk lights strung like a necklace along the shore. Without speaking, they turned toward Neptune, the slow tide shushing the edges of the city's noise.

"Somehow, I think our money's dry by now," Tim said, trying for lightness.

Laura smiled, looping her arm through his. "Then we're officially solvent. For tonight."

"Well, if we find a souvenir shop, I'm getting a 'I died and all I got was this lousy T-shirt' shirt."

Laura gave up a smile as they rounded the last corner with a shared held breath, bracing for the sight of an idling locomotive, a door yawning open, a summons they couldn't refuse.

It wasn't there.

They exhaled together, a small, relieved laugh slipping out at the same time.

"We still have time," Laura said softly. Pleasantly.

"Still free to do what we want," Tim answered.

They wandered back to the boardwalk, moving at a slower, looser pace. A bench faced the ocean; they took it like it had been saving their spot. Tim slipped an arm around her, and she leaned in, fitting neatly into the curve of his shoulder. The waves lapped and retreated in a rhythm that matched their breaths. A few late joggers passed, the soft tap of shoes on planks fading behind them, while far out, a ship's lights drifted, small and steady as prayer candles on the water.

Darkness deepened until the horizon and sky became one black-blue ribbon. Their words thinned to quiet hums of contentment, then to silence. The day's heat bled from the boards beneath their bare feet, and sleep found them; slow, simple, welcome.

Sometime in the deep middle of the night, the air shifted. Not colder - warmer, in a dry, breathless way. The faintest metallic tang brushed Tim's tongue. The boardwalk lamps gave a brief, almost apologetic flicker.

A train whistle blew.

They stirred, blinked, and sat up together, the sound settling over them like a summons they both recognized. Despondently -

there was no other word for it - they stood and made their way away from Neptune, from the bistro, from the beach, from the beauty of the day they had just spent together.

Where there had been nothing, there was now a train, the door open as if it had been waiting all along.

"Back to our regularly scheduled nightmare," Tim spoke somberly.

At the threshold, they turned to look back, as if to seal the day behind their eyes: the bright noon ocean, wet socks on a bench, music at the edge of the surf, ice cream running down their wrists, a kiss in hot sand. Tim swallowed; Laura squeezed his hand.

Was this a promise of a brighter future? They certainly hoped so.

They stepped aboard. The door slid shut. The night held its breath, then let them go.

CHAPTER 5

The Toll

When they stepped back onto the suicide train - a place they had both hoped never to see again – it felt like they were slipping into a nightmare that masqueraded as comfort. The air was cool but carried a faint metallic tang, and the seats gave off their usual worn-leather scent. There was no station platform, no tracks stretching away into the distance, only the impossible sense that the train existed in some void, untethered from any real location at all.

Laura slid into her seat with a small sigh, her body sinking into the cracked leather. Tim followed, his weight hitting the bench with a thud that rocked it slightly. Despite everything, despite the unspoken knowledge of where they were and why, they both carried a fragile glow from the day's earlier reprieve. Their laughter and loosened spirits from the bar still clung to them, like a warm aftertaste.

"I had a great day," Laura murmured, curling into Tim's side. Her hand sought his and found it easily, squeezing as if to make sure he was still there, as if he weren't some kind of mirage waiting to fade when looked at too closely. Her head rested on his shoulder, and he let out a long, contented breath.

"I did too," he said softly, leaning his cheek against her hair. "I hope we get to do it again." He hesitated, then smiled faintly. "You know... my dad used to have this elaborate model train set in our basement. We spent hours down there, playing in that miniature world. I used to imagine the stories of the people in the cars..." His voice trailed as the memory pulled him backward, but Laura's fingers gave him a reassuring squeeze, pulling him gently back to now.

Tim chuckled. "This... train is nothing like that one."

Laura laughed quietly. "You mean your train wasn't full of people who—"

"Not once," Tim interrupted quickly, though with a touch of sadness. "Most of my passengers were on their way to vacation, not... well, wherever this goes."

"Good," Laura teased. "A kid like that would've worried me. Straight out of a Stephen King novel."

Tim grinned. "If we get out of here, maybe I'll write it down. The Boy Who Controlled His Passengers. Sounds more Twilight Zone than King, however."

"Either way, creepy," she said.

He nodded. "Agreed."

The clack of the wheels became their only conversation for a while, until Tim broke the quiet. "Hey... why are the railroad tracks angry?"

Laura groaned without answering, bracing herself. "I was happy with silence, you know?"

Tim laughed, "Yeah, well, we can't always have everything. The answer is because people are always crossing them."

Laura rolled her eyes, but her lips fought a smile. She shook her head, "Don't tell me you're one of those. Are you going to be like that when you're a dad?"

Tim squeezed her hand. "You bet. My dad had the corniest jokes, and I'm carrying the torch. But don't worry. They get better." He paused and shrugged, "Well, they might not, but I do." Tim gave Laura a look filled with implications.

"Good," she murmured, reaching up and planting a kiss on his cheek. "I think our kids would like that."

That warm, impossible thought barely had time to settle before a voice sliced through the car like a blade, a voice that wiped out the sweetness as if stomping it under a soiled boot.

"Well, well, well... isn't that sweet?"

The mocking drawl slithered down the aisle, and both of them turned to see *him*, the sharply dressed man from before, the one who had studied them as they slept during their first ride. His entrance was theatrical, deliberate - as if the shadows escorted him in with pomp and circumstance.

Arms extended slightly at his sides, he moved with unsettling grace, a grin stretched across his face - too wide, too fixed. It had the twisted glee of a comic book villain, something between a showman and a threat - more Joker than gentleman.

Tim instinctively tightened his grip on Laura's hand, the protector in him rising fast. "Who the hell are you?" he snapped, flicking his chin toward the demonic figure beside the man. His voice was low and edged with steel, but the spike in his pulse betrayed his calm.

The man's smile curved into something colder, and his eyes narrowed in mock confusion. He leaned in, voice dropping to a growl that dripped contempt. "I was about to ask you the same... damn... question. Who *are* you interlopers on my train? Why *are* you trespassing?"

Tim tried, nervously, to hold his ground. "We didn't ask to be put here. How could we possibly be trespassing?"

The man tilted his head, his salt-and-pepper hair catching the dim light. "Well, I certainly didn't invite you. And this..." he swept his arm toward the car with theatrical disdain "this... every last inch ...is mine."

His hands moved suddenly, snatching Laura's wrists and shoving them toward Tim's face. "Ohhh," he drew out the word with mock realization. "Now I understand how you got here." His gaze sharpened. "What I don't understand is why you're still so... real." His eyes narrowed, then flared red for just a breath. "You certainly aren't like the others."

The air seemed to tighten, pressing in around them. His smile dropped. He began to grow then, not metaphorically, but monstrously, his frame stretching upward as if reality itself bent to accommodate him.

His shirt pulled taut across his shoulders, buttons threatening to burst. When he spoke again, his voice was like gravel-soaked in flame. "Nobody rides my train for free."

Tim tried to keep his tone level, his hutzpah at the maximum. "Do you take cash? It might be a little wet..."

The man's jaw unhinged in an unnatural grin that was far too wide, the hinges groaning like a rusty gate. Three rows of razor-edged teeth revealed themselves in the dim light.

"Smartass," he said with relish. "Good. I like a challenge."

He leaned down until his breath was hot against Tim's face. "I don't accept cash here... boy. No, your payment here is simpler... just a little bit of your soul... a slice of your joy... a fracture of your love. Keep your soggy paper." His voice dropped to a whisper that seemed to somehow scrape bone. "I'll keep taking, piece by piece, until... you beg me to end it."

The car flickered. Shadowy passengers appeared in the seats around them. Some famous, recognizable, most anonymous, but all broken. The addicted, the hopeless, each frozen in a silent scream.

The man strolled the aisle, whispering to each, dismissing them with a casual flick of his wrist until they dissolved into nothing.

When he returned, his size had receded, his shirt once again immaculate, but his eyes still burned with fire. "You've made it further than most, love birds. Let's see if you can survive what comes next. And if you do..." His smirk deepened, and he straightened his shirt with a tug downward. "I might even enjoy the ride."

Tim's hand found the back of Laura's head, shielding her as she pressed into his shoulder. His voice stayed steady, even as his insides churned. "We'll take whatever comes. What we've found - you can't break."

The man chuckled darkly. "You may think so, but what you've found is not love, my friend."

He leaned in, teeth glinting again. He pointed a crooked finger at both of them. "What you've found... is *hope*. And hope," he whispered as he demonically curled his fingers into a fist, "is the easiest thing to starve... especially here."

He was gone as quickly as he came. Only the hum of the rails remained.

Tim exhaled slowly. "Let's not talk about that."

Laura's voice was small, her nerves on edge. "I just want to get off and be with you, Tim. He can't change what I feel, but... I'm frightened. I know he'll be back, and I don't know how we'll ever get free of him."

He met her eyes. "We keep moving. Together."

She nodded back, wiping at her tears, trying to force a smile. "Okay."

And as if their pact had triggered something, the brakes shrieked and sunlight poured through the windows.

Tim stood and held out his hand, a dignified smile on his face. "Our meant-to-be awaits, my lady."

Laura took it, forcing a smile. "Here's to our meant-to-be. It had better be good."

Tim smiled at her. "Well, for this part of the ride, let's pretend we know what we're doing."

The door opened with a metallic squeal.

CHAPTER 6

Wedding Bells

What greeted them when they stepped off the train was something between a chapel and a reception hall, draped in soft amber light that filtered in through high-arched windows. The light poured down like honey through cathedral glass, gilding the polished floor and scattering soft glints across ivory drapes and floral accents that seemed to shimmer with breathless anticipation. The room was quiet and expectant, as if it had been waiting just for them. A silence not of emptiness, but of reverence - like the hush before a symphony begins, or the moment when breath is held before saying "I do."

Tim turned toward Laura and stopped. His foot hovered above the next step, forgotten. Everything in him stilled, caught between heartbeats.

His eyes widened with a mixture of awe and disbelief. It was as if he were seeing her for the first time, though he had never stopped looking. She stood radiant in a gown of ivory lace, the bodice delicately shaped to her frame, the hem trailing like fog across the polished floor. The lace caught the light like frost on morning grass, each delicate stitch echoing something eternal and ancient, like the whisper of vows yet to be spoken.

All remnants of the previous day had vanished, the wetness of the ocean, the sand, the strangeness of it all - but the memories remained in his mind. They clung to him like the smell of salt air and the echo of waves, gentle and cherished. Fond memories that he prayed would never fade. In their place stood a vision he had never dared to imagine. The kind of beauty that didn't just surprise you, it undid you. His heart swelled with love so intense it rose through his chest and nearly choked him with its fullness.

Laura stared back, her breath caught in her throat. She had forgotten how to breathe, how to blink. Gone were the tattered clothes and bruised weariness. Tim now wore a black tuxedo that clung to him with tailored ease, a crisp white shirt, and a matching bow tie, with a red cummerbund completing the transformation. He looked like someone carved out of a memory she'd once tucked away in secret - refined, certain, achingly handsome. He looked like he had stepped out of some forgotten dream of hers – a 12-year-old dreaming of her big day.

They both laughed softly, the sound a shared release of wonder and nerves. A fragile laugh, stitched with disbelief but anchored in something real - like wind rustling through leaves that have just seen rain, longing to take flight.

Tim swallowed, glanced down at his tux, then back up with a half-smirk. Even now, he couldn't help himself. Falling back on old habits, he tried to break the tension with a joke. "If this is the afterlife, it's got great tailoring."

Laura smiled and squeezed his hand. Warmth pulsed through her fingers into his, like electricity softened by her grace. "Don't be nervous, Tim. We're going head-on into this... whatever it is. No hesitations. No regrets."

Tim nodded in agreement. "No hesitation. No regrets." He repeated it like a vow, not to her, but with her.

He reached out to touch her hair with his right hand when he noticed something there on his pinky. A shimmer caught his eye; unexpected, almost sacred. A ring more beautiful than any he had ever seen. Three curved bands of gold, woven together and intertwined with diamond adornments. It looked as though it had been forged out of light itself, delicate, eternal, undeniably meant for them. He slowly took it in his other hand, smiled at Laura, whose eyes had gone wide and whose smile was beyond compare.
She looked as though she'd just remembered something her soul had always known.

Then, he knelt before her and slowly lifted his eyes. There was no hesitation in the movement, only reverence, like bending before something holy. There was no struggle for words here. "Laura Palmer, we may have just met in the grand timeline of existence, but we both know... this is our meant-to-be. We've spoken the words, made that commitment. I will go to the ends of the... wherever this is and beyond with you - so now I'm asking you: will you marry me?"

Laura's breath caught. Time stuttered around her. For a moment, everything else, the walls, the train, the world, faded. She took his hand. "We don't understand any of this," she said, her voice trembling. "But I think I love you. I'm terrified about all of it, but I think it's true." A tear left her eye and found its way down her cheek.

She took the ring from his hand, slipped it onto her finger, and kissed him. The moment their lips touched, the room seemed to breathe again. "I promise to be kind to you. I promise to care for you. I promise to love you."

Tim's eyes glistened. "I know you will," he whispered. His voice cracked with certainty and awe as if the answer had always been yes. "And I promise the same for you. Always."

She laughed, a free, musical laugh, and tugged free from his hand. The sound of her laughter rang out like a bell on a still morning; pure, uncoiled joy.

Laura looked across the room to where a large mirror was mounted on the wall. "I need the mirror!"

Tim smiled, the weight of their journey beginning to dissolve. It lifted from his shoulders like a coat he no longer needed to wear, set aside for the summer. Whatever this place was, between life and death, now and then, it had offered them this moment. And Tim would take it.

Laura rushed to the mirror, her train following in lazy arcs across the floor. The fabric whispered across the hardwood as it swept behind her, as if reluctant to let her go.

Tim followed more slowly, giving her time to herself, but when he reached her, his hand found the small of her back, drawing her into a kiss until she pulled away with mock outrage.

"Whoa! You're not supposed to see me before the wedding," she teased, flicking him away in a dramatic gesture, a little too reminiscent of the man in white. Her hand froze mid-air for a heartbeat, the joke brushing against memory like a shadow through glass.

Regret flickered across her face. "I'm sorry, Tim. I didn't mean to conjure up that..."

Tim grinned. "It's fine, but it's going to cost you one kiss."

Laura sighed, kissed him again, and pointed across the room. "Now... go."

As Laura examined herself in the mirror, Tim wandered toward the altar - if it could be called that. There was no pulpit, no choir loft. Just space. It was simply a table draped with linen, bathed in soft pink and violet light. The colors shimmered like the final hues of dusk, a palette caught between the setting of one world and the rise of another.

There was no adornment, no cross, no crescent moon, no Star of David. Just a peace sign hanging on the wall. A quiet declaration, not of religion, but of longing. Of the unclaimed. The not-quite-there. A symbol for souls who didn't quite belong anywhere. The kind of souls who still hoped for something more. The ones who just wanted peace – ultimately just peace – in their lives.

Beside a speaker on a black tripod sat a small electronic organ. It looked oddly out of place and perfectly right all at once. Its polished wood and familiar shape pulled at Tim's memory.

The memory didn't come gently; it gripped him, sweet and sharp as a chord struck too soon. His mother's music echoed in his head: Vidor, Beethoven, Bach... all soaring through sanctuaries, climbing rafters, kissing stained glass. Notes fluttered in his mind like doves startled into flight.

He reached out, brushing the keys. The plastic was cool beneath his fingers, yet carried phantom heat from a thousand long-ago hymns. He inhaled deeply, and the scent of varnish - faint, nostalgic - filled his lungs. It was the smell of pews and Sunday clothes, of bulletins folded neatly in laps, of a childhood that hadn't entirely let go.

He looked back. Laura was still adjusting her hair in the mirror, framed by lace-draped tables with glowing lanterns. The lanterns pulsed softly, casting star-shaped patterns that danced across the floor like memories made visible, and for a moment, everything was still.

Then Laura gasped and spun around. Something had changed. It had begun.

The room was suddenly full: guests, music, laughter.

Not in a burst, but a breath. As if they had always been there, waiting to be seen.

Tim's mother, radiant, impossibly alive, sat at the organ, and his mouth dropped open in shock. Tears burned in Tim's eyes when he saw her. They came quickly, blurring the moment into watercolor. He didn't fight them because the moment nearly crushed him with joy, ache, and disbelief. His heart didn't know what to do with it all, except break open wider.

Her music wrapped around him, lifting and grounding him all at once. The sound was warm, familiar. Not just a melody, but a heartbeat he thought he'd lost forever. But right then, doubt crept in. It was quiet but persistent, like a cold draft through stained glass. Was this a memory? A hallucination? A trick?

The pain of his past rushed in:

His mother's accident.

His father's descent.

His spiral - slow, unrelenting, into the darkest depths of depression.

These weren't shadows. They were anchors.

But this time, he caught it.

This wasn't just a memory. This was a test.

This was the man in white's influence. *He* did this. He was taunting them, trying to break their resolve.

And that realization struck like a bell: clear, cold, liberating.

It gave him strength.

He straightened, drew a deep breath, and turned, not to run, but to face whatever this was with both feet planted.

Laura stood across the room, glowing, not just from the lighting, but from within. It was as if her very cells had begun to hum with light. It was a beauty Tim had never seen before.

Not surface beauty.

Something deeper.

Something earned.

Something discovered and rediscovered with each passing moment.

Her smile bloomed, and he crossed to her.

No more questions. No more fear. Just the answer walking toward her.

His eyes scanned the room. Behind him now, he saw that the room wasn't just full of guests. It was filled with *witnesses*: people he knew, people he didn't. Faces from the past - moments past. Each one was like a lantern lit in his memory - some flickering, some steady, all present.

Laura caught his eye, and she smiled. Her eyes sparkled with tears, just like his. But in hers, there was no fear. Only affection. Only yes.

Tim lifted his hand and gave a small wave, not a casual wave, not a "hey there" kind of thing, but a wave filled with layered meaning. It said: *You are the most beautiful woman I've ever seen. You are the light inside my dark and weary soul. I'm all in. If you are - I'm all in.*

She met his gaze, her head cocked slightly, an expression so tender it buckled his chest. It was the kind of look that unraveled every defense, every doubt. He knew, without words, that she felt the same way. It was the kind of understanding that transcended sound. The kind that had to be earned through loss.

Laura stood at the mirror, still half-lost in awe, running her fingers along the folds of the dress, the sparkle of the ring that had been afforded to her.

The fabric felt too fine. The diamond too brilliant. The moment too overwhelming.

Was she really up for this? Did she deserve this? Could two broken souls really build something whole?

And then came the question beneath all others: how was it even possible?

Laura looked around the room, and then her gaze shifted. Tim's family was on one side, and hers, what there was of it, was on the other. The family dynamic on her side of the room was drastically different than Tim's.

Where Tim had known a mother who was loving, nurturing, and present, Laura's life had been shaped by a series of brief, impersonal stops through the foster system.

There were people who knew *of* her, maybe even liked her for a while, but no one who had ever anchored to her heart the way a true family should. She had grown up with borrowed roofs and borrowed affections, always temporary, always one foot out the door.

Then she saw him.

A familiar face emerged from the crowd like a lighthouse cutting through fog, stepping forward to show his influence.

Uncle Tyrone.

He stood tall and unmistakable, a weathered mountain of kindness wrapped in a dark suit. His face hadn't changed: broad, lined, full of calm strength. His eyes still held that soft amber warmth that once made her feel safe in a world that had rarely offered such comfort.

It was always a curious sight: Tyrone, an African-American man with a booming baritone and larger-than-life presence, beside a young white girl clinging to his arm like he was the only truth left in the world. But blood had never mattered to him. And it had never mattered to her either.

He had seen her, not just looked, but truly seen her.

Her memory recoiled, however, as another figure flickered into her mind.

Horatio Reed. The Reverend.

A man praised from the pulpit, adored in the community. He had been her legal guardian, a Baptist preacher with the velvet voice of persuasion and the polished air of righteousness. But beneath the robes and reverence had lurked a darkness she could not have named at the time, only feared.

He had not adopted children out of grace. He had done it out of hunger, twisted, unspeakable hunger, and Laura had been one of his victims.

The memory clutched her without warning: the slivered moment weeks before her thirteenth birthday, standing in her room, changing. She had felt the weight of eyes that should not have been there. The look that wasn't paternal. The intent was not accidental.

It hadn't been a misstep. It had been a beginning.

And then came Thanksgiving.

That memory blazed like a brand in her mind, plates clattering, laughter simmering under the surface, and her shrinking like a ghost in every room he entered. She had tried to disappear into corners, afraid even of her own breath.

Tyrone had noticed.

He told her later that it had clicked in an instant. He had heard rumors, whispers, half-believed, but the moment he saw her face, that wide-eyed silence, he knew.

That day, he had taken Horatio outside. A single punch. A black eye. A warning growled between clenched teeth.

And then he had packed Laura's things without waiting for permission and brought her home, where warmth and safety lingered a little longer.

He hadn't been able to keep her, system rules, bureaucratic nonsense. He had wept when he said goodbye, believing he'd failed her. But he hadn't.

His love had never left her.

It followed her from house to house, hardship to hardship. Through court hearings, cold dinners, and lonely birthdays. His love was the lifeline she clung to, even as others faded into the background of a fractured past.

And now, he was here. Smiling at her across the room. Steady as ever. Just like that Thanksgiving Day.

Laura's breath caught in her throat.

He had been her beacon. Her safe harbor. Her definition of "good."

And now he stood here, bearing witness to the start of a new life – if her prayers could somehow be answered in a place such as this.

A tear spilled silently down her cheek. No blood relatives sat in the chairs behind her, no ancestral anchors like Tim had, but it didn't matter. Not anymore.

She *wanted* this. Not just the day. Not just the dress.

She wanted *him*, Tim. With her whole, broken, healing heart.

She yearned for joy. For home. For the warmth of ordinary days wrapped in love and laughter. They were two people, lost and found. Pieced together not by fate, but by grace. With Tim by her side, they would build something new. Something sacred. Not perfect, but *theirs*.

As Laura looked toward Tim, the opening chords of Richard Wagner's "Bridal Chorus" filled the space. Familiar. Iconic. Suddenly intimate.

It was time.

She had no father to give her away, but she had something better. She turned to Tyrone, and their eyes met. Her heart swelled with gratitude so big it felt like it might spill from her chest. She extended her arm toward him, her smile trembling with a mix of joy and memory.

And Tyrone, blessed Tyrone, didn't hesitate.

His shoulders squared, eyes misted, and he stepped forward with reverent pride. He took her arm, steady and sure, and together they walked toward the altar.

One step at a time.

Into hope.

Into healing.

Into love.

The aisle, lined with the soft flicker of candlelight from star-punched lanterns, stretched before them like a dream. Each gentle glow cast warmth onto the faces of those gathered, guests who watched in reverent silence, some with glistening eyes, others with wide, heartfelt smiles. But Laura barely noticed any of it. Her world had narrowed to one man: Tim.

As they reached him, standing tall at the altar bathed in soft hues of violet and pink, she turned first to Tyrone.

"This is Uncle Tyrone," she said, her voice catching as emotion surged up through her chest. "My rock and strength in a very hard time in my life." She swallowed against the rising tide of tears. "He... he saved my life."

Tim stepped forward and extended his hand. The handshake was firm, respectful, steady, and sincere. Tyrone's eyes narrowed slightly, not with suspicion, but with the weight of someone entrusted with a treasure.

"I only have one question," Tyrone said, his tone low and measured.

The air seemed to shift. Tim felt it... not pressure, but importance. He hesitated for a beat, not out of doubt, but because he didn't want to falter. This man, however ethereal, meant everything to Laura. His blessing was more than symbolic; it was sacred.

Tim straightened his back and found his footing in love, not fear. "Okay."

Tyrone rolled his neck slowly, as if warming up for a truth that needed to be spoken, then locked eyes with Tim. "You love her?"

There wasn't a breath of hesitation.

"With all my heart and soul," Tim replied, voice clear and unwavering.

Tyrone nodded, the tightness in his jaw softening into a warm, tear-lined smile. He looked at Laura, then gently placed her hand into Tim's. "Then you take care of this girl, ya hear. She hasn't had much good luck in her life. I hope with all my heart you're the one who'll bring it to her." His large hand patted theirs with tenderness before he turned and slipped quietly back into the crowd, disappearing into their warmth.

"Thank you, sir," Tim called after him, then turned to Laura with a smile, patting her hand lightly. "Uncle Tyrone?"

She returned the smile. "I'll tell you about it some other time."

Together, they turned to face the altar.

Tim supposed nothing should surprise him in this strange place anymore. But when he turned around, he was caught off guard once again.

Some people carve out space in your soul and never leave, not just memories, but guiding imprints. And there, standing at the altar, was Pastor Brian, Tim's childhood pastor. A man with a square jaw to match his crew cut, but whose smile always reached his eyes. He wasn't theatrical. He wasn't loud. He was simply present. A steady, grounded shepherd who made you feel known and safe.

Tim's knees nearly gave way. Emotion rushed into his throat and stole his voice.

"Pastor Brian," he whispered. "It's so... so very good to see you."

The pastor held a small wedding service book in his hands. His voice, as always, was calm and sure. "Timothy Wentz. Look at you. It's certainly good to see you as well."

He stepped closer, eyes glancing briefly across the assembled crowd, his tone dropping as he leaned in, acknowledging the surreal nature of it all.

"I'm guessing that since you're here with me, you are..." Pastor Brian trailed off gently.

Tim shook his head, glancing at Laura before returning his gaze.

"No, sir. I didn't think I'd ever be able to say this... my life has been so full of..." He paused and took a breath. "But I'm not dead. At least I don't believe I am. Let's just say I'm... looking for redemption."

Pastor Brian studied him for a moment, then smiled wider, eyes soft with something like pride. "Well, there is plenty of that here... if you know where to look."

Tim turned toward Laura, who waited patiently, her smile calm and knowing. "Pastor Brian, this is Laura," he said. "Would you please marry us?"

The pastor's face lit up, lines deepening around his eyes like the creases of a well-loved book.

"Well, Tim, I haven't done a wedding in many, many years," he said, surveying the glowing room and the sea of expectant faces. "But I suppose once you're a pastor, you're always a pastor. Even here."

He raised his voice gently, letting it roll through the hush with warmth and authority.

"Friends, let us join Tim and Laura in marriage, so that together they may learn the love, peace, and happiness of a family. Together, let us help them find their way to the redemption they are searching for."

He opened the small book slowly, reverently, as if every word inside had just become sacred again.

"Let us pray..."

Tim bowed his head. A soft breath slipped from his lips, a release of weight he hadn't realized he was still carrying. He squeezed Laura's hand. In her eyes, he found a quiet certainty. And in that certainty, he felt the stirrings of something he hadn't known in years: peace.

As Pastor Brian led them through their vows, Tim held Laura's gaze. He saw more than beauty there. He saw determination, courage, and a flickering vision of a future they could build, one brick at a time.

He realized, with bone-deep conviction: they could do this.

No matter how uncertain the road ahead, no matter how surreal the journey so far had been, they could walk it together. Step by step. Creating a home. A family. A love neither had dared dream of before.

A love that just might save them both.

The ceremony, as it turned out, was brief and unembellished, yet profound. Their vows were spoken with trembling voices but unwavering eyes. It felt less like a performance and more like a promise carved into the very walls of this place.

And when Pastor Brian finally said the words they longed to hear, "Tim and Laura, I now pronounce you man and wife," the eruption of applause stunned them.

The joy echoed across the room, louder and more radiant than they'd imagined. The crowd, once just vague outlines of memory, now shimmered into a sea of faces; some known, some long forgotten, others deeply missed.

It was as though all the souls who had shaped them had gathered, not just to witness the union, but to bless it. A holy chorus. A cosmic amen.

Hand in hand, Tim and Laura stepped forward, their smiles pure and wide. The happiness between them didn't just show; it radiated, vibrating in the air like music you didn't even know you needed.

For a fleeting moment, it felt like a small victory over the man in white. That strange, chilling conductor from the train. As if marrying in this space was an act of rebellion. A reclaiming of something sacred.

Or perhaps - perhaps it was part of his plan all along.

But in this moment, none of that mattered.

They had each other. And that was enough.

The organ began to play again, the unmistakable grandeur of Purcell's "Trumpet Voluntary" swelling throughout the hall. Tim's mother was back at the instrument, alive in her music, brilliant in her playing. She was as good as she had ever been, her fingers dancing across the keys with the command of a seasoned artist.

The newlyweds made their way toward the back of the room, husband and wife at last. Each step felt surreal, like walking through a living dream stitched together from fragments of the best memories they never actually had; echoes of joy they longed for but never lived.

When they reached the rear, Tim turned for one last look.

His mother sat poised at the organ, the melody still rolling from her fingertips, but something was changing.

The music began to shift. Smoothly. Seamlessly.

The classical tones melted into the steady, soulful rhythm of Motown. The stately air transformed into something warmer, groovier, alive with a new kind of joy.

The organ itself shimmered, its polished wood morphing into a sleek DJ table lined with small monitors and blinking lights. The long, brass pedals vanished, replaced by a row of digital inputs pulsing with light.

And sitting in place of Tim's mother was a dark-skinned man with a round face, a head full of a proud afro, and glorious mutton chops that framed his jawline like a monument to the 1970s. He held a pair of headphones to one ear, either cueing up the next song or preserving the sculpted perfection of his 'do.

From speakers now hidden in every corner of the room, the unmistakable opening chords of Stevie Wonder's "You Are the

Sunshine of My Life" rose and swelled, turning the dream into a full-blown celebration.

Some of the guests, now freed from the solemnity of the ceremony, began to sway and dance. Their faces lit with uninhibited joy. No more sadness. No more grief. Only movement. Only music.

Tim and Laura looked at each other, bemused and delighted.

Who was that DJ?

Before either could ask aloud, a voice from behind answered with warm familiarity.

"That's my brother, Jerry. Back in the day, he was a good DJ."

They turned to see Uncle Tyrone again, smiling fondly at the man at the controls.

"Yeah, DJ work was a nice part-time job for Jerry. Kept him outta trouble. Helped pay the bills. Good thing too. When he was left unattended..." Tyrone laughed softly, shaking his head. "Whoo wee, that man was a rabble-rouser."

He stopped, the laughter fading slightly into nostalgia.

"Sad. It was lung cancer what got the best of him. Not a kind illness. Not kind at all." A tear shimmered in his eye, but his smile remained steady. "Man loved himself the seventies, though."

Laura and Tim chuckled softly, their eyes flicking back to Jerry, who was now bobbing to the beat with a look of deep, righteous satisfaction on his face. A man in his element, even here, even now.

Laura stepped forward and wrapped her arms around Uncle Tyrone's neck, her voice filled with emotion. "I'm so glad you're here, Uncle Tyrone. You're the only one in my life who ever..."

Tyrone gently pulled back just enough to look her in the eye.

"I know, girl. I was always there for you. It was wrong what *Reverend* Horatio did to you. There was never nuttin' reverent 'bout that man."

His voice darkened like a thundercloud passing overhead.

"Still, I'm glad I got you outta there. My only wish was that I'd had the finances to keep you with us. You know that, right?"

Laura's eyes filled again. She nodded, unable to speak, her tears sliding down her cheeks in quiet streams. "I know. It's fine. I know."

"I didn't have the wherewithal to do nothin' for you, sweetheart. I had to let you go." He looked down at his shoes, his voice thick with emotion. "If only I knew then..."

Before she could respond, a loud clattering of plates and utensils broke the moment.

They both turned toward the sound, watching as silverware skidded across the table and guests started lining up near a buffet now materialized where pews once were.

Tyrone, ever the mood-shifter, gave a hard clap and headed in that direction. "Awesome! Food!"

Laura and Tim followed.

The buffet table was filled with the warm, mouthwatering smells of roasted chicken, slices of beef in rich brown gravy, rigatoni and meatballs, a medley of colorful vegetables, peas, beans, carrots, and corn - and fresh rolls with butter. The scent alone felt like home.

But something felt... off.

Laura's mood shifted.

A flicker of something dark passed over her face as her eyes scanned the guests, *certain* guests, gathered near the food.

Her smile vanished. Her breath hitched.

And then, like a sudden storm, her rage returned.

Laura's eyes locked on a man and a woman who had been dancing near the buffet, both dressed in dull, unremarkable clothes. Their presence sliced through her joy like a blade. They didn't belong here.

She marched toward them with fire in her stride, her heels clacking against the floor like war drums. Her face was red, flushed with fury.

"You," she snarled, pointing an accusatory finger. Tim stayed behind, frozen in confusion.

The couple froze mid-step, startled.

"This is *my* wedding," Laura shouted. "And you aren't invited."

Tim instinctively stepped forward, but something in her eyes stopped him. She wasn't unraveling. She wasn't breaking down. This wasn't collapse, it was combustion. It was necessary. Righteous.

"You did nothing for me while I was a child except ignore me and collect your paycheck from the state," she seethed. "When I was sick, you had no medicine. When I wanted comfort and felt alone, you locked me in my room and waited it out."

Her voice was shaking, but not from weakness. From rage, finally unshackled.

"Get the hell away from me!"

With the same flick of the hand the man in white had used to dismiss the souls on the train, she banished them - foster parents gone wrong.

The room hushed. A few guests turned their heads; others kept watching. No one intervened.

Laura spun around toward another man now, one who had just been filling his plate but now looked as if he were trying to blend into the tablecloth or hide behind his plate of rigatoni.

"And you," she barked, her eyes narrow and deadly, "you think because I'm a woman I'm your... your maid?"

She stepped toward him like a storm at sea, unrelenting and full of thunder.

"Clean this, cook that, don't stop until you're too exhausted to move, then do it again tomorrow!"

Her voice cracked as it grew louder.

"GET. OUT."

The man dropped his plate. Food cascaded to the floor, spilling around Laura's feet. She didn't flinch.

With another flick of her hand, he vanished.

Then her eyes caught another couple, scruffy, rough-edged, underdressed in flannel and jeans, and she charged toward them like a lioness cornering her prey. They backed up immediately, fear etched deep in their expressions.

"Oh, there's no escaping, you bastards," she hissed. "You think you can hit me? Punch me? Drive your cigarettes into my arms to punish me?"

Her voice rose into a scream.

"You think you can pull my hair, spit on me, call me vile, hurtful names? I was FIFTEEN YEARS OLD!"

The couple tried to retreat further, their backs hitting the wall, but Laura didn't slow. She launched into them, punching, kicking, screaming in feral release.

They were trapped, unable to vanish. Tim's eyes went wide, but he didn't move. Even he knew this had to happen. That this fury wasn't destruction, it was survival. It was Laura reclaiming herself.

Finally, breathless, spent, she stepped back, hand flicking once more. They too vanished, like ashes caught in a sudden gust.

Then she turned slowly and came face to face with someone else.

A portly, dark-skinned man was hunched in the corner of the room, trying to shrink into himself, silently praying for release. But Laura had seen him.

Horatio. Tyrone, standing near Tim, muttered grimly, "Horatio." His voice was hard as iron.

Tim instinctively stepped forward, but Laura spun toward him, her eyes ablaze with something he hadn't seen before, something eerily close to the man in white. He backed off.

Laura turned back to Horatio, fists clenching and unclenching.

Her voice dropped to a dangerous calm. "And finally, you... Horatio."

The man trembled, trying to appear smaller.

"It's a good thing you had a brother-in-law who saw what you were doing and saved me," Laura continued, stepping closer. "Because otherwise I was going to kill you."

She paused. "I had this knife under my mattress. You remember that, don't you? The one your wife would use to chop meat?"

She pivoted and walked to the serving table, retrieving a **carving knife** from beside the beef. She held it up elegantly, like a queen displaying judgment, and turned back toward him.

Horatio's face was locked in fear. He couldn't move.

Her voice was fire and ice. "Do you know what foster care is supposed to be, Reverend?"

She reached him, the knife's tip resting lightly against his chest.

"Foster care is supposed to be about *love*. About *safety*. About *hope*. About giving a child structure, purpose, and peace."

Her hand twitched. The blade sliced through his chest.

A section of him vanished, swirling away in a shimmer of light and dust.

Her tone rose.

"Foster care is NOT fondling!"

She slashed across his arms. They dissolved, shimmering like a mirage.

Horatio shook uncontrollably. His eyes screamed.

"It's NOT scaring young girls into doing what your wife wouldn't do!"

She slashed an X across his chest. His torso began to dissolve, flickering, the room visible through him.

He began to tremble as his form broke apart, like glass under pressure.

"And it's NOT scarring a girl so badly she can't even have a normal relationship for the rest of her life."

Laura raised the knife and paused. Her final words were a roar of righteous rage.

"It's *not* for taking advantage of young women!"

She plunged the knife into his groin.

Horatio convulsed, a scream forming but never reaching his lips. What was left of him shimmered and vanished in a final, silent explosion of dust and light.

Laura stood still for a moment, holding the knife.

Then she dropped it with a clatter, her body shaking.

She turned to Tim and gave a soft, exhausted smile. "There," she said softly. "Now you know my story."

She walked calmly toward him, her steps slower now, her body shaking, but not from fear. From *release*. From power reclaimed.

She leaned in close and whispered, "Let's dance."

Tim reached for her, pulling her into his arms with tenderness. "You are..." he began.

Laura pulled back just enough to meet his eyes, a half-smile on her lips. "Batshit crazy?"

Tim shook his head, smiling through emotion. "No. Sad. Wounded. And... beautiful."

Laura rested her head on his shoulder. Closed her eyes. Breathed.

From the loudspeakers, Frank Sinatra's golden voice filled the air, crooning the timeless words of *"The Way You Look Tonight."*

Tim's heart trembled.

As the music wrapped around them, his eyes scanned the room, and he found him - his **father**.

Standing at the edge of the dance floor. Watching.

She followed his gaze, saw the man, and smiled. "Let's finish the song. Then you can introduce me to your family. I can't wait to meet them."

Tim nodded, eyes suddenly misty, the weight of years and healing and hope catching him off guard.

He never wanted to let go.

Frank Sinatra's voice swelled around them, velvet smooth and heartbreakingly sincere: *I love you... just the way you look tonight...*

As the final note lingered like a sigh, Laura pulled Tim into a long, loving kiss. It wasn't urgent. It wasn't for show. It was a sealing, a soft cementing of everything that had just happened.

Then, true to her word, she took his hand and led him across the room.

Waiting for them was Tim's family.

Tim's mother, who had since stepped away from the organ, now stood arm-in-arm with his father. Her face was radiant, lit from within by a joy that shimmered like morning light. His, calm and strong, bore the steady gaze of a man who had seen eternity and made peace with it. Beside them, drink in hand and grin already in place, was Uncle Max; loud as ever even in silence, his presence a gravitational pull of laughter and warmth.

Tim's heart was pounding. These were the faces he had longed to see in life, and here they were now, on the other side of death, reunion, or whatever this place truly was.

He approached slowly, like a nervous child unsure of how much joy he was allowed.

When he reached them, he looked into his father's eyes, then gently released Laura's hand and wrapped his arms around the man in a tight, breath-stealing hug.

"Timmy..." his father whispered. The sound of that name from those lips nearly undid him.

"I see you took that step."

Tim trembled. His voice faltered. "I didn't think I had a choice anymore, Dad. When you left me... my world caved in. Nothing I did, nothing I tried, was ever the same again. I saw you in every room, in every decision. I thought I could never do anything without you." He stepped back, wiping tears from his face with the back of his sleeve. "But... in retrospect, I guess..."

His father reached out, placing a firm hand on Tim's cheek. "If there's anything good that's come from it, Timmy, it's this." He gestured toward Laura, then back to Tim.

"I hope you two find happiness. True happiness. This place," he gave his head a slight tilt to the side as if considering, "it's not so bad, really. There are periods of nothing... and then there are reunions. And those are *amazing*. Like this reception. Everyone who ever knew you gets to come somehow. And then..." He looked around, smiling. "Then something like this."

Tim leaned in, lowered his voice, his eyes scanning the room as if the answer was hiding there in plain sight. "I don't think we're dead, Dad. Not truly. There's this train and..."

His father held up a hand gently. "I get it. You don't have to say anymore."

And somehow, Tim believed him.

There was something in his father's tone, like he already knew more than he could say. It was as if he had peeked behind the curtain and simply smiled at the mystery.

"So," he straightened and continued, looking between the two of them, "if this is some kind of in-between, then I hope you figure out what needs to be done..." he looked directly at Laura and smiled. "...and have a very happy life together."

Tim took his father's hand and shook it with gratitude. "Thank you, Dad. That means everything to me. So far, it *has* been happy. Very happy. I'm so in love with her, it hurts just thinking about life without her. She's unlike anyone I've ever met."

His mother, beaming with pride, reached out and gently joined her hand to theirs. "It's unlike anything you'll ever experience again."

Tim turned to her, his voice breaking. "Mom..."

He leaned in and hugged her tightly.

"You haven't missed a beat on the organ," he said through a half-laugh, half-sob. "Your playing still fills my soul."

Part of him wanted to ask why she had run that stop sign. Why had she changed his world forever? But he didn't.

Instead, he took a deep breath and stepped away.

"I love you, Mom," he whispered into her ear.

Then he turned to Uncle Max.

Max greeted him with a big bear hug and a slap on the back. "Timmy! My favorite nephew. How's it hangin', old chap?"

Tim laughed and shook his head, the warmth of Max's energy infectious.

From behind them, Tim's mother shook her head in mock scorn. "Max, what, are you British now? Is this the British side of heaven?"

That brought a loud guffaw from Tim's father, who pulled her closer. "You still got it, Rose."

She looked up at him and smiled as if they were young again.

Ignoring the teasing, Tim turned back to Laura and reached for her hand. Together, they walked over to the group.

"Mom, Dad, Max," he said, nodding to each. "I'd like to introduce you to my bride. This is Laura."

Each one of them spoke her name back to her softly, nodding gently in approval.

Laura stood with her hands nervously folded in front of her. "It's so nice to meet the three of you. Tim has told me so much about you. I only wish it were under different circumstances..."

She trailed off, unsure of how to finish the thought.

Max, ever the disruptor, chimed in, "Us being dead and all!" He laughed heartily.

Tim's mom and dad exchanged knowing glances, then turned back to Laura with tender expressions. They smiled at her warmly.

Tim's father stepped in first and hugged Laura, followed quickly by his mother.

Afterward, Laura took the initiative and hugged Max, too. "I wish I had more family like you three," she said softly. "The love you have for each other... it transcends even death."

She glanced toward Tyrone across the room. "I have Uncle Tyrone, of course. But beyond that..." She ran a hand across her face to catch the tears forming again, then smiled and swallowed the tears away. "No regrets, right? We have to boldly step into the future. Isn't that what you always say?" She looked at Tim's father.

He nodded gently. "Take one step. Be brave and..."

"Right. Take one step."

Tim's mother stepped forward again. "Laura, I know you and Timmy have both had hard lives. But I can see it in your eyes, you're going to be good for each other. I know you'll take care of each other. You'll make each other happy."

Laura turned to her and placed her hand over hers. "I promise I'll take care of your son, Mrs. Wentz."

She was interrupted by a soft smile and a correction.

"*You* are Mrs. Wentz now, my dear."

Laura glanced down at her ring and smiled. "Oh... I guess I am."

She looked up again and placed her hand on Rose's shoulder. "This is just the beginning for us. I hope, someday, we'll get back to the real world and..."

Tim's father took her hand. His voice lowered to just above a whisper. "It'll happen. Trust me. It will happen."

Laura smiled, brushing away a fresh tear. "I hope so."

As the conversation paused, the music shifted once again.

Etta James' soulful voice filled the room, wailing the iconic lines of "*At Last.*"

Tim's father turned to his wife. "Would you like to dance, dear?"

She laughed. "Henry, I thought you'd never ask."

They made their way across the room, slow and graceful.

Just before they reached the other side of the floor, Henry stopped and shook hands with a **striking blonde-haired man** with shoulder-length hair and a faint, knowing smile.

Tim's eyes narrowed. "Who..."

But before he could finish, Laura took his hand and gently pulled him toward the dance floor.

"Care to dance, Mr. Wentz?"

He looked one more time toward the blonde stranger, who had already disappeared into the crowd. Then he turned back to Laura and smiled.

"I would love to dance. I'd love to do *anything* with you, Mrs. Wentz."

And so, hand in hand, they stepped into the swirl of music, motion, and memory. Around them, the family danced. Love danced. Life danced.

And for the first time in either of their lives, everything felt right.

The mysterious blonde-haired man that Tim's father had greeted vanished as quickly as he had appeared. Nothing more was said. Tim tried to bring it up once as he and Laura circled the floor, arm in arm, calling out to his father, but his father had smiled, walked over, and placed a hand on his shoulder. Quietly, he spoke, "Timmy, not yet."

The moment passed, tucked away like a folded note in a pocket, destined to be opened later, when the time was right.

For the next hour or so, the hall was filled with dancing, laughter, and warm embraces. Soft golden light shimmered across the guests as they swayed to music that Jerry served up, enveloping them like sunlight through stained glass. Tim and Laura were never alone for long; friends old and new came to greet them. Some faces Tim recognized instantly: aunts and uncles from long-ago Christmases, childhood friends from forgotten playgrounds, distant cousins with familiar eyes.

Others were strangers, but their smiles were knowing. It was as if they had once walked through the same dream.

Each guest embraced them warmly, whispered blessings, then vanished. Softly. Quietly. As if they had only ever been made of light and memory.

Eventually, only a small handful remained: Uncle Max, Uncle Tyrone, and Tim's parents. Jerry still sat across the room, engrossed in his music.

Max was the first to break the stillness. He ambled up with an easy swagger, arms wide, eyes bright, voice booming like it always had.

"Timmy, my friend. It's been so good to see you." He wrapped Tim in a bear hug, lifting him slightly off the floor with a jolly grunt.

"I'll be waiting for your return. We'll have some good times, then." He pointed with a mischievous glint. "I'll show you the sights!"

Tim chuckled, his heart aching with affection and nostalgia. "I'll make sure of it, Uncle Max."

Laura stepped forward and hugged Max warmly, resting her head against his shoulder for a brief moment. "Just... not too soon, okay? We have a lifetime to share first."

Max leaned back, holding her at arm's length with a cheeky wink. "Gotcha. Y'all take care, now."

And then he vanished, as if he'd been swallowed into the warm ether that wrapped the room.

Uncle Tyrone stepped forward next. Tall and broad-shouldered, he moved quietly, his steps heavy with unspoken emotion. He wrapped Laura in a hug so deep and fierce it nearly knocked the breath out of her.

His voice, low and gravelly, now softened like the rumble of thunder beyond the horizon.

"It's gonna be okay, girl. Timmy's a good man. I like him. He's gonna treat you right, take care of you, and be a man to you."

He held her there, then whispered, so low only she could hear, "I can rest peacefully now, knowing you're safe."

Laura couldn't find words. Her throat clenched, eyes swimming. She could only cry into his shoulder, whispering, "Thank you," over and over again, like a prayer.

Tyrone held her a heartbeat longer, then pulled back and smiled.

And just like that, he too was gone.

Tim and Laura stood in silence, their fingers interlaced. The spot where Tyrone had stood shimmered faintly before returning to stillness.

The silence stretched until Tim's father cleared his throat.

"Well, Timmy..."

Tim turned toward them slowly, not ready.

His eyes met theirs, his mother's gentle smile, his father's proud but wistful expression, and he felt a pressure in his chest so tender it almost dropped him to his knees.

Laura squeezed his hand. Her touch was a quiet anchor, keeping him upright.

"Now you know, dear," his mother said gently. "We're okay. That should mean something to you. That should give your soul rest."

Tim nodded, slowly. The weight of her words pressed into him, reshaping the cracks inside.

"And now," his father added with a soft smile, "you can let go a little. Alright?"

"I'm not alone anymore," Tim said, his voice thick and unsteady. "I know you're always there with me. And I have Laura."

He looked at her, then back to his parents.

"When this train ride ends and..."

"Life begins," his mother finished for him, her voice like the hush of leaves in the wind.

Tim nodded. "Life begins. Then I'll be okay. More than okay."

His mother stepped towards Laura and gathered her into a gentle embrace, warmth radiating from her like the final glow of candlelight.

"You take care of our boy."

"Oh, you can count on it," Laura replied, just starting to return the hug, but her arms met only air.

They were gone.

A shared breath left both their lips. The moment folded in on itself, and they were alone. They glanced across the room, and even the steadfast Jerry was gone – yet the music still lingered.

Tim looked at Laura, wonder in his eyes, the unspoken still humming between them.

"Guess they had to go."

"Guess so," she whispered, resting her hand gently on his chest.

Then she rose to meet him, pressing a long, lingering kiss on his lips. It wasn't urgent. It wasn't performative. It was a promise, sealed with breath and skin. Her arms looped behind his neck. His arms circled her waist.

And in that kiss, the reception hall shimmered.

At first, neither of them noticed.

Not until the walls blurred and the lanterns faded, and something altogether new took their place: a breathtaking hotel room, drenched in warm light.

Tim blinked, dazed by the sudden shift, and broke off the perfection of the kiss.

"Not very subtle, are they?"

The room was glowing with quiet luxury. A golden table lamp cast soft light across the oak nightstand. Candles flickered gently on a linen-covered table beside a wide-paned window that opened onto a sunset too perfect for Earth - deep purples and fiery oranges dissolving into a serene, cerulean sea. White sand sparkled far below, as if the stars themselves had gathered for a beachside celebration.

A golden comforter was pulled back invitingly on one side of the bed. A spray of flowers crowned the table. A lush plant stood watch in the corner, peaceful and still.

Tim turned to Laura, still holding her hands. Her eyes sparkled as they met his.

"Once, a man met a genie..."

Laura smiled, stepping closer to the bed.

"Tim, are you going to do these jokes forever?"

He grinned, softly, shyly, his heart too full to speak.

"Good," she whispered. She kissed him again, her fingers tightening slightly behind his neck.

"Still, can we please consummate this marriage first?"

Tim didn't answer.

He didn't need to.

They undressed each other slowly, reverently, with a kind of sacred patience. Neither looked away. Not once. Not even when tears caught in the corners of their eyes.

And in the golden hush of that timeless room, they made love. Not just in passion, but in healing. In joy. In release.

Two broken people, finally made whole.

Never had such a magnitude of happiness come to two souls who had known so much sorrow.

CHAPTER 7

The Full Ride

The newlyweds slept deeply beneath the heavy velvet of night, the darkness in their hotel room thick and undisturbed. Outside their door, however, a different kind of darkness lingered; more sentient, more aware. The hallway was silent save for the faint hum of flickering electric light, and in its shadows stood the man in white.

He leaned against the wall just outside their door, one foot up, arms crossed casually, as if he were simply waiting for a late elevator. But the wry smile on his face betrayed a more sinister satisfaction. It was a smile carved from secrets. A smile steeped in knowledge meant only for him. As time went on, it twisted slowly into something worse: a grin pulsing with dread and inevitability. His pale fingers tapped an eerie rhythm on his bicep, like a metronome to someone else's doom.

Then, without a sound, he pushed off the wall and walked away, footsteps absorbed by the carpet as if the hotel itself were complicit. The lights continued their flickering above until he was... gone.

Inside, Laura woke with a sudden gasp, her eyes flying open as her body lurched upward in bed. Her heart pounded, racing in irregular rhythm like tom-tom drums on a battlefield, every beat an alarm. Her head throbbed so violently she half expected it to crack open, the pain a brutal hammer behind her eyes. Sweat soaked through her nightshirt, an unfamiliar garment clinging to her skin like a second, damp layer - one she didn't remember ever owning, as if her body had been through a war in her sleep and woke wearing someone else's pain.

The air felt too heavy, pressing down on her chest with invisible weight. Her lungs worked double, drawing in thin, unsatisfying gasps. She sat up slowly, jerky and uncertain, as though gravity couldn't make up its mind. Her muscles protested, her nerves frayed and overstimulated. When she finally accomplished the herculean task, she looked around, eyes scanning a room that felt both foreign and familiar.

The darkness was complete, save for a thin wash of light from the bathroom, a glow she had insisted on before sleep. In that faint halo, she could make out Tim's still form beside her. He was sleeping soundly, chest rising and falling in peaceful cadence, his expression untroubled.

A grim realization slithered into her mind, cold and unwelcome. A brief panic attack crossed her mind, not in theory but in fact, already blooming in her chest like a toxic flower. What was I thinking? she asked herself. I married this man I just met. A couple of days ago, I was in my bathtub... crying... with a razor in my hand.

Her hand moved instinctively to Tim's back, tracing the curve of his spine, the defined muscles beneath his warm skin as if looking for affirmation for her actions. Her fingers trembled as they touched him, but slowly, beautifully, she began to relax - completely and ultimately relax, as if her entire body rejoiced with his touch.

Still, despite the sudden certainty, the doubts continued their quiet siege. Who am I to deserve this? she thought. I don't know anything about him... except that he tried to kill himself, too. Sure, his parents seemed great, and his uncle... she smiled. Who could ever forget Uncle Max? She knew it would be a while before she would.

Laura sighed, a long, audible exhale that rippled through the silence. Tim didn't stir. Yet, her thoughts grew heavier, darker, as if the sigh had summoned the weight of them. Am I crazy? I feel like I'm going crazy.

Laura finally rose from the bed and padded softly toward the bathroom. Her bare feet made no sound against the carpet, but her shadow flickered and warped in the dim spill of the light. She closed the door gently behind her, the soft click echoing louder in her ears than it should have. She leaned over the sink, gripping it with both hands, knuckles pale and locked tight as she stared into the mirror.

What she saw stopped her breath cold.

It was the first time she had truly seen herself since arriving in this in-between place. Her reflection didn't look like her. Her reflection was pale and gaunt, the skin around her eyes shadowed and drawn. She looked older, years older than the woman she remembered being. Her eyes were rimmed with exhaustion and sadness, the color in them dulled by grief. The vibrancy of her wedding, if it had ever been real, was gone, leaving only a hollow kind of beauty.

Why is he with me? she wondered. I was beautiful once... maybe just yesterday. But now? I look like someone death has already come for.

Turning, she moved to sit on the toilet lid, but a sudden twist in her gut forced her to her knees. Her stomach flipped violently, an uncontrollable rebellion rising. She barely had time to lift the lid before vomiting into the bowl. The dinner from the reception, the warm, comforting food, roared back in acid waves, turning her joy into shame.

When the retching ended, she wiped her mouth with the back of her shaking hand. Her legs wobbled as she stood slowly, weakly, returning to the mirror. Her face was even worse now, flushed, streaked, haunted. *Much* worse, she thought.

Before she could spiral deeper into the pit, there was a knock at the door.

"Laura?" Tim's voice was kind, concerned, muffled through the faux wood. "Are you okay?"

The doorknob clicked slightly as he peeked through the crack.

"I'm fine," she snapped. "Can you just... please... leave me alone?"

Tim didn't budge. He heard the way her voice trembled, the fragile, brittle edge it carried. And, even though he had only been with Laura for two days, he knew what this tone meant; he'd used it himself during his darkest moments. Despair. He opened the door fully and crossed the room to her.

She was still leaning on the sink, facing the mirror, her face pale as parchment and just as thin. He wrapped his arms around her without hesitation.

"Honey... are you sick?"

The answer was obvious.

Laura turned in his embrace and clutched him desperately. Her sobs came in choking waves, the kind that seized the throat and shook the whole body.

"Why are you with me?" she cried. "I don't understand how you can be with me. I'm not beautiful. I'm not... anything."

She pushed away, held out her wrists like accusations.

"Look," she demanded. "LOOK at me! I'm old and tired and haggard and scarred and sad... why the hell would anyone want this?"

Tim took her hands and held them tightly, ignoring the trembling, the scars, the anger.

"Laura," he said gently. "Where is all this coming from? At the wedding, you kept saying this was meant to be. Over and over."

"I was trying to convince myself. Trying to convince both of us." Her voice was barely more than breath, but he heard her. He felt her. "I don't know why I deserve any of this," she whispered.

Tim wrapped her in his arms again and pulled her tight. "Laura, of course, you're beautiful. I've come to love you so deeply it's consumed me. Even if you weren't beautiful, and you are, I'd still be with you. Because I believe in this. I *also* believe we're meant to be." He kissed the top of her head. "And scars or not, I'm one lucky guy. Because I get you."

"You're right, Tim," she whispered, her voice calming, slow, and warm. "I do. I do believe the meant-to-be part. It has to be. I have to have that to hold on to. It's just... I just... when I'm not right next to you... when I can't hold you... the fear starts creeping in."

She filled the glass on the counter with water and rinsed her mouth, wiping her face with a towel in slow, methodical swipes, grounding herself in the moment.

"I guess I had a panic attack in the dark. I kept thinking, what if I lose you? What if I'm left alone again? What if I... what if the man in white..." she glanced at her wrists.

Tim took her hands again, and he could feel her shaking like a taut wire. He tried to calm her, speaking with certainty, conviction in every syllable.

"You're not alone anymore, Laura. And you never will be. You're with me. And we're going to stay together. Whole. Happy. Strong."

Laura nodded, the tears now gone, and she wiped at her cheeks to erase any sign of them. She led him quietly back to the bedroom. They sat together on the edge of the bed, and she placed her head against his chest. His arms circled her instinctively, an unspoken vow.

"We're going to be okay?" she whispered.

"We're going to be okay," he whispered back.

She nodded. "Okay."

Her head rose and fell with his breathing, and just before surrendering to rest, she reached out, placing her hand lightly against his chest; not to wake him, not to hold him, just to feel him there. That quiet contact was all it took. The storm within her settled, the edges of her panic dulled by warmth and presence. She didn't need to speak. She just needed to touch.

And in that stillness, she finally let go.

Sometime in the night, without noise or fanfare, the luxurious hotel room dissolved into memory. The flicker of candles, the golden bedding, the velvet hush of honeymoon comfort, it all vanished. In their place came the low, rhythmic clack of wheels on steel and the ever-so-slight sway of a moving train.

Tim and Laura slept soundly, curled together on one of the long wooden benches in the dim, musty car that had first carried them into this strange journey. Her cheek rested on his shoulder; his arms held her gently, protectively, as if some part of him knew the dream had ended.

And in the seat directly across from them, *he* returned.

The man in white sat with one leg crossed over the other, his chin resting lazily in his palm, watching them with a narrowed gaze and faint, unreadable smile. Shadows played along his sharp features as he studied the slow, synchronized rise and fall of their breathing.

"If all goes well..." he murmured to himself, the tone smooth but tinged with amusement. His eyes caught on Laura's hand, which now rested protectively against her belly. The corner of his mouth twitched upward. He lifted a pale hand and gave a single snap.

"Perfect."

Laura's eyes flew open with the sound, her body jolting as if yanked from sleep. Her breath caught in her throat, and her surroundings, the cracked upholstery, the dim overhead lights, the scent of old smoke and rust, told her instantly something had changed. Something felt wrong, but she couldn't explain it.

"Wait... we're... back on the train?" she said, voice hoarse with confusion. "What happened to the..."

"The suite? The wedding cake? The music?" the man in white interrupted smoothly. "Your last stop was finished." His voice dripped false politeness. "And with your... transgressions," he nodded at her wrists, "you bought a pass for the full ride. Did you really think you'd just get married and live happily ever after?"

He twirled a hand through the air in an exaggerated, mocking flourish, like a magician unveiling a tired trick.

Laura's face was frozen in disbelief. Tim stirred beside her, disoriented. She shook him gently. "Tim... honey. Wake up."

Tim blinked, then sat up, rubbing his eyes. "What the hell...?" His gaze darted around the train car. "How are we back here?"

Laura pointed, jaw clenched. "Don't ask me. Ask *him*."

Tim sat up straighter, tension rising in his shoulders. "What's your deal? Why can't you just leave us alone?"

The man in white smiled wider, his expression laced with condescension. "Why so angry, Timmy, my boy? I was merely explaining to your bride that thanks to your combined... colorful histories..." He rolled his neck with performative flair. "You both qualified for the extended journey. You're going to just love the adventure."

He stood then, arms spread wide like a ringmaster in some macabre circus. "And because you two are... let's face it, *interesting*. Most souls are dull, predictable, and terribly disappointing. They give up at the first flick of the wrist. But you? No, no. You're outliers. Interlopers. Wild cards. Which is why..." He paused, eyes narrowing. "...you shouldn't exist here."

Tim rose to his feet. "Well... maybe there's a reason we do. Maybe we were put here for something bigger. You think you know everything, but you don't know why we're *still* here, do you? Maybe this is our second chance. Maybe we're meant to finish what we left undone."

Laura added firmly, matching Tim's courage, standing in front of her seat. "You act like you're in control, but you never ask. You never once asked if *we* were *sure*. Not like you do with the others. That's how I know... you don't know either."

For a beat, the man in white was silent. Then his grin returned, slow, serpentine, hideously stretched. His voice dipped to something gravelly and cold.

"Now *you* listen to *me*... you interlopers. *I. HAVE. CONTROL.*"

He shook with rage for a brief second, eyes glowing yellow, teeth clenched, then smoothed his jacket and smiled again as if the storm had passed.

"But... I think I'll *use* that control to give you something special."

His gaze dropped, unmistakably, to Laura's stomach. And lingered. Far too long.

Tim's heart froze. Then understanding crashed into him. "Are you serious?"

The man in white's eyes gleamed. "Be careful what you do when you *consummate* a marriage. Some things... *stick.*"

Laura turned to Tim, breath catching in her throat. "Is he saying what I think...?" Her fingers clutched at his arm, trembling, but her eyes were wide with wonder.

The man in white stepped backward, already fading into shadow. "I told you you'd love your next stop. See you soon, lovebirds!"

His laughter echoed like a bad dream as the train screeched to a halt. White light spilled through the windows, and both Tim and Laura were thrown back into their seats by the force of the stop.

They sat up slowly, dazed.

Laura looked down. Her hand moved across her abdomen. A warmth bloomed under her palm, quiet and impossible.

"Tim..." she whispered, her voice trembling. "Is this... really happening?"

Tim's mouth opened, closed, then opened again. He finally nodded. "I don't know how... I mean, I *know how,* but... I guess it is."

She grinned and laughed, half in shock, half in joy.

Tim offered his hand. "Shall we?"

Laura hesitated. "But what if... what if he's still in control, just like he said?"

Tim squeezed her fingers. "Then we'll be braver than he is."

"I'm afraid."

"I'm with you. Always."

They stood, walked to the door, and stepped off the train and into their future.

***

The cold hiss of hydraulic brakes faded into the steady beeping of machines. When the doors opened, fluorescent lights bloomed above them like a sunrise filtered through hospital glass. The air smelled sterile: alcohol wipes, clean linens, and something vaguely floral. Everything was already in motion. Nurses in blue and green scrubs moved efficiently, almost reverently, as if they'd been expecting them for hours.

Tim blinked in confusion. Laura clutched his hand tightly, her eyes darting across the room. A birthing bed appeared from nowhere, rolled in by a soft-spoken doctor who didn't seem surprised to see them.

"You're right on time," she said, as if reading from a script. Her voice had an accent Tim couldn't place. Indian, maybe? Kind. Rehearsed. "Please, lie back, Mrs...?"

"Wentz," she whispered, offering a tiny smile at her new name.

"Correct. Laura Wentz," the doctor repeated gently, as if she already knew and was just confirming the fact for whoever recorded things in the cosmos.

Tim helped her onto the bed, and she lowered herself slowly, still unsure if any of this was real, the swiftness almost more than she could bear. Nurses bustled in harmony. One adjusted the monitors, another dimmed the overheads, setting the room aglow with golden lamplight. Someone handed Tim scrubs, which he hastily threw on over his clothes.

Laura squeezed his hand with sudden urgency. "Tell me one of your corny jokes."

He looked startled, then smiled. "A wife asked her husband, 'Why is there a different baby in our crib?'"

Laura raised an eyebrow, waiting.

"Because," Tim said, "you told me to *change* him."

She laughed, a full, bright laugh that filled the sterile room with warmth.

"Thank you," she said, her voice catching in her throat. "Our child is going to love you."

"And you, Mom," Tim replied softly, brushing a strand of hair from her forehead.

A contraction gripped her body, sudden and sharp, and she arched back instinctively. The doctor moved closer, calm and composed. "You're almost ready. Just relax and let nature take its course."

Laura nodded, tears gathering at the edges of her eyes. Not from pain, at least not only pain, but from wonder. From the miracle of it all. From the terrifying beauty of being on the edge of something *new*.

She gripped Tim's hand like a lifeline.

Outside the delivery room, the world remained unknowable. Whether they were in a dream, or death, or somewhere beyond, none of it mattered now. Because inside this room, in this one incandescent moment, life was coming.

And no one, not even the man in white, could steal that from them.

CHAPTER 8

Miracle in Motion

No longer surprised by the magic that seemed to transport them from place to place, but possibly still a bit frightened, Laura eased back down in the bed after another contraction. Her body moved slowly, uncertainly, like she didn't fully trust the ground beneath her.

Tim placed himself nervously in a padded blue chair to the left of her. The chair had wooden arms and was glossy and worn at the corners. His anxious tapping created a faint, steady rhythm that made Laura uneasy. It echoed in the quiet like a ticking clock.

"Tim, honey..." She placed her hand on his, and he briefly stopped, looking at her with a tight smile that didn't quite mask the nervous tremble beneath it.

"I'm sorry. I'm just so... ugh! This is so unexpected, is all."

She patted his hand again, a silent signal to stay grounded. "I know it's unexpected and we're both nervous, but I'm sure these fine doctors and nurses have done this before."

She looked up at the doctor, searching her face for reassurance. Tim must have been doing the same, because the doctor placed a warm, steadying hand on Laura's leg and spoke in an accent that matched her deep brown complexion and wise, ageless eyes.

"Back in the day, honey, I was the best. You're in good hands."

The confidence in her tone wrapped around them like a warm blanket. Tim looked amazed and confused as he took in the room; clinical yet soft, real yet surreal. On the wall across from him was a whiteboard listing just one name: Wentz. The only one that mattered.

Next to it, an electronic monitor came to life as a nurse, efficient and gentle, attached sensors to Laura's belly. The whir and beep of machines created an eerie symphony of welcome and warning. Behind the bed was a hardwood headboard, elegant, cherry-stained, an intentional effort to add warmth and erase the usual sterility of hospital rooms. Scalloped lights adorned each side like little halos, casting golden puddles of calm into the space.

Another monitor came to life beside her, lines and numbers dancing like cryptic poetry. As the nurses gently worked around her, adjusting wires and tubes, Tim's curiosity broke through his caution.

"I'm sure you were the best around, but is there much call for delivering babies here? I mean... you know?"

The doctor turned, slow and deliberate, and looked at Tim with a smile that didn't quite reach her eyes. The edges of it were cool, not unkind, but firm. "Mr. Wentz, I go wherever I'm needed." She let the words hang in the air like smoke. Then, with a flick of her eyes back to Laura, she added in a voice almost too quiet to catch, "You'd be surprised at what goes on in places you've never even imagined. The universe is a *very* big place."

Tim studied her stare for a few more seconds, caught in the gravity of something bigger than he could name. Then he backed off, exhaling. "Fair enough. I don't know how I got here, where the train came from, the station, the beach, the wedding... so, I guess it's safe to say I don't have a clue about this either. Sorry for the interruption." He held up his hands in surrender.

"It's quite all right," replied the doctor, the corners of her mouth softening. She returned to her place at the end of the bed and sat on a small rolling stool, positioned like a watchful guardian. "Your baby is almost here, Mrs. Wentz. It won't be long before you'll be a very happy family."

Laura looked at Tim and grabbed his hand, squeezing it as she did so. Her fingers were cold, her palm damp with nerves. "We are already very happy. A baby..." And then she froze.

It hit her. All at once.

Yesterday - if yesterday had any meaning here - she had been thin. Flat stomach, fitted dress. And now... she was anything but.

Her wedding gown had vanished, replaced by the stark vulnerability of a hospital gown. The magic of the wedding, so vivid only moments ago, now seemed to fade from her mind like the last wisps of a dream, replaced by...

A contraction slammed her so hard that she screamed, the sound sharp and sudden. Her hand clamped down on Tim's with desperate strength, and he let out a yelp of pain.

"Tim," she breathed methodically, trying to imitate the rhythm she'd seen in so many movie scenes. "We're having a freaking baby here."

Tim chuckled, his voice tight with disbelief. He tried not to wince. "I know that, honey." He began to panic and went to the first place his mind wandered to when he was stressed. "Say, did you ever hear the one..."

Laura screamed again as the next contraction peaked. In between sharp breaths, she gasped, "Is this... really the best place for a..."

The doctor smiled beneath her mask, only her eyes visible, calm, amused, and steady. "Take a short break, Mrs. Wentz. Oh, you two are such a cute couple. I think you're going to make excellent parents."

Laura looked up at Tim, her expression softening into a smile that radiated through the pain. Love. Pure and unshaken. But there was no time to bask in it. The doctor leaned forward again, hands slipping beneath the sheet like a pianist preparing for a symphony.

"Now take a breath, here comes another..."

Laura screamed again, louder this time. It caught Tim off guard once more, and he instinctively braced himself, his hand already red and throbbing from her grip. He kissed her forehead, which glistened with sweat, and whispered close.

"It's going to be fine, Laura. I won't let anything happen. Besides, we need some good news. The love of a child will help us along on our journey."

"Our journey to where?" Laura screamed, her voice breaking as the pain doubled. Her eyes searched his face, desperate for assurance, for anything steady to hold on to. The contraction faded, and she collapsed into him, sobbing. "Timmy, please tell me everything's going to be okay. What if something goes wrong? What if he takes the..."

Tim placed a trembling finger against her lips, holding her. His other hand rubbed her back in slow, small circles. His voice was soft but firm. "Shh. It's all going to be okay. Everything will be okay."

She spoke into his shoulder, her words muffled but laced with fear. "What if it's not, Tim? What if this isn't our meant-to-be, but a cruel look at what we missed instead? What if it's all some life review... showing us what we didn't take advantage of and then we're shipped off to... somewhere else?"

Her sobs came harder now, her body trembling. "Tim..." Her voice faltered, thin, distant. Her eyes lost focus and instead searched the wall as if looking for something else. "I can hear them again." She blinked hard, as if trying to focus through water. "Voices. Like before, when I first, you know. They're calling my name. I - I think... they're trying to pull me back. Back there. In my bathroom..." She cried then. "I don't know if I'm ready, Tim. I want to be with you!"

Tim pulled her close and kissed the crown of her head, whispering, "I'm sticking with the meant-to-be. Let's focus on that. Anything else would be against all we hold..."

Laura screamed again, falling flat on the bed, erasing all of the previous conversation. "Tim! The baby is coming right now!"

The doctor returned to her seat with practiced ease, her mask stretching as her eyes crinkled into a smile. "Oh, you sure are right, dear. It's here. Are you ready?"

Laura grabbed Tim's hand tighter than ever and turned to him with wild, blazing eyes.

"I know I'm supposed to be screaming at you for putting this baby inside of me, telling you I never want to touch you again, lashing out at you in pain, but I'm not going to do that. I realize now that I don't care if this is a preview of what's to come or insight into what we missed. I don't want to be saved back there, not yet. I just want to take the chance and be with you. I just want to... take... the... steeeeeep!"

Another contraction hit. Laura screamed, her entire body tensing as she bore down. The doctor's voice rose calmly over it.

"Wow, this one is in a hurry to get here. There's not going to be much more pain, just one more push. This baby's ready to make an appearance."

Two nurses moved in sync on either side of Laura, helping her sit up, steadying her shoulders. The doctor leaned forward.

"Annnd push."

Laura bore down with everything she had. The doctor's voice rang out. "Okay, I can see the head. Almost here. Just one last time!"

Tim's breath caught in his throat. He looked at Laura, radiant and raw, a warrior and a mother all at once, and kissed the back of her hand.

The nurses guided Laura forward one more time.

Laura pushed.

And then, the release.

The doctor's voice softened. "Okay, you can stop pushing. The baby's here."

Laura collapsed onto the bed, shaking, every muscle spent. Tim leaned over her, kissed her again, and wiped her damp brow.

"You did great, babe."

But Laura's eyes, glassy and wide, turned toward him. "The baby," she said urgently, her grip on his hand like iron. "Is it okay?"

Tim's heart lurched. He turned quickly to the doctor, breath held.

And then, a smile.

The doctor lifted the vernix-covered child gently and placed her on Laura's chest. The room shifted. Time, as it was, stopped. Laura's arms folded around the tiny, squirming miracle, her hand softly tracing the curve of her back.

"You have a brand new baby girl, Mrs. Wentz. Congratulations. What's her name?"

The couple exchanged a bewildered glance.

Laura chuckled, her eyes locked on her daughter in a mixture of wonder and disbelief. "We haven't really..."

"There really hasn't been time," Tim added.

"Well, I understand," the doctor said, moving to leave the room as the attendants cleaned up. "It happens more often than you would think. Especially in places such as this." She looked around at her surroundings as if that explained it all to the new family. As if that explained all that they had gone through to get there. "Still... you have time. Just keep your daughter there on your chest so you can bond. Let the connection grow. You both have had a busy day." She waved her hands in a lazy circle. "Somehow, however it happens, the name will come to you."

Laura held the baby close, tears pouring forth. Her chest rose and fell in uneven breaths. "Tim, look at this. Look at everything we... we almost missed. We wasted our lives on troubles, on frustrations, on... on things that didn't matter. Mine on *people* that didn't matter."

"Mine on letting go," Tim added.

"Instead, we should have been more focused on *ourselves*," Laura continued. "On what made *us* happy."

Tim nodded, overcome. His throat was tight with emotion. "I know. Still, we never had each other before this, so I'm saying we didn't know. We couldn't have known." He gently rubbed the baby's back and kissed her head, then kissed Laura. "She's such a beautiful miracle. I never realized there could be something like this."

"Me either," Laura laughed lightly, though her voice trembled with awe. "Not just the baby. Everything. I just... I just really never want it to end. Is it possible to grow so in love with someone you've only just met? Or maybe because everything else is moving so fast on this train, our feelings are too?"

"I know what you mean. Everything that's happening really does feel... I know I say it too much, but meant-to-be. I love you deeper than anyone I've ever loved. And now her. It's all so..."

The baby cried, making sure the parents knew she was around.

Tim and Laura both laughed gently, and Tim rubbed her back. "It's okay, honey. Everything's going to be okay. Mommy and Daddy are here."

He looked at Laura with a smirk. "We really need to give this baby a name. We can't just call her honey forever. Anyone in your life you want to name her after?"

Laura smiled. "The only person in my family I ever liked was Tyrone. Not a great name for a girl."

"No," Tim chuckled. "She'd hate us. Especially when she starts dating. No boy wants to date Uncle Tyrone."

Laura laughed. "Let's not get ahead of ourselves. We have a long way to go before dating. So, Tyrone is out. How about you?"

"My mother's name was Rose," Tim replied questioningly.

Laura tilted her head, and her eyes sparkled. "I heard your father call her that. Such a beautiful name. And a perfect tribute."

She looked down at the newborn and kissed her head, her voice soft and laced with tears. "Welcome to the world, Rose Wentz. We're glad you came. Mommy and Daddy are ready to see what you're going to do."

Tim beamed, whispering into Laura's ear. "I've never been happier."

"Neither have I. Thank you."

Tim was running the back of his finger along Rose's cheek when a nurse returned. "Sorry, folks, but it's time to take the baby. We need to clean her and run some tests, get some measurements. You'll see her again soon, I promise."

Laura handed Rose over, speaking softly. "Bye, Rosie."

The nurse smiled. "Oh, so you decided on the name then? Rosie?"

"Well, Rose," Tim corrected.

The nurse nodded and turned. "Well, it's a beautiful name for a beautiful girl. Let's go get you cleaned up, Rose. Tell Mommy and Daddy you'll see them later."

As if on cue, Rose gave a soft coo, and the three of them offered up a small chuckle.

Tim held Laura's hand quietly until another nurse entered. "Your room is ready now, Mrs. Wentz."

Laura got into a wheelchair, and Tim helped her settle into a smaller, cozier room. The lights were dimmer, the linens softer, as if the room itself understood what they needed. Neither one of them questioned that this was all happening in a place that shouldn't even exist... but somehow did. When Laura was settled, Tim tucked a blanket around her and kissed her forehead. Laura smiled and closed her eyes.

Tim found a chair and a blanket of his own. It had been a good day.

Somewhat rested, Laura stirred hours later. Almost immediately, as if she had been anticipating her waking up, a nurse placed Rose in her arms. The warmth of the infant against her chest sent Laura's senses reeling. She sat up, brushing her eyes, blinking away the fog of sleep.

"It's time for Rose to eat," the nurse said gently, with a knowing smile.

Tim stirred too. "Hello, Rose. I missed you." He got out of his seat and crossed to kiss her on the cheek. He brushed Laura's hair aside with gentle fingers. "Is there something you want me to do?"

Laura smiled up at him. "No, Tim. I'm afraid you don't have the right parts. Just hand me that small blanket."

Tim passed it over. Laura covered herself and Rose, then looked up at him.

"Thank you, Tim. This is the best gift I've ever had. The best day I will *ever* have."

Tim squeezed her hand and kissed her forehead. "Me too. I can't think of anything better."

A comfortable silence filled the room as Rose fed. Laura watched with love in her eyes, and Tim sat nearby like a proud father, perfectly content in the world around him, no matter how strange it was.

The day moved forward with more naps, more feedings, and more quiet bonding. They spoke little, needing only presence. As evening shadows began to stretch across the floor, Laura dozed and whispered, "Do you think we'll wake up here in the morning?"

Tim shook his head sadly. "No. I'm pretty certain that won't happen. I think we still have further to go. But I know one thing."

"What's that?" Laura asked sleepily.

"We will do it together. As a family."

Laura offered a soft smile. Sleep took her.

Tim followed, his head resting gently on her chest.

CHAPTER 9

The Shape of Us

Rose's cry ripped them out of sleep and into the dull greyness that pressed in from all sides. For a moment, it felt like a dream, but the steady clacking of wheels against rails snapped them back into the harsh reality - once again, they were trapped on the train.

"Well," Tim muttered, his voice rough as he wiped at his dry mouth. He stretched, bones popping in protest, trying to unknot the stiffness that had settled into his neck. "Back on the train."

"I see," Laura answered, her tone soft, heavy with sorrow. "Together, though." She looked down at Rose in the grayness of the train car. "All of us."

In the dim shadows of the car, she fumbled with her blouse until she freed herself and guided Rose to her breast. The baby latched on instantly, her wails fading into the small, rhythmic sounds of nursing. Tim averted his gaze, embarrassed, eyes fixed forward as though the iron darkness of the aisle demanded his full attention.

"Do you think he'll come again?" Laura's voice trembled as she finally dared to look around the car herself.

Tim answered without hesitation. "I'm as certain of that as I am of anything else." He glanced at Laura's face. She appeared genuinely concerned. "Don't worry. I won't let him touch the baby." His words were matter-of-fact, but there was steel beneath them.

Laura leaned her head against his shoulder, her eyes falling closed. Together they rocked in time with the swaying car, her body moving gently with Rose as she nursed.

For a while, the silence stretched between them, broken only by the groan of rails and the hush of breath. Tim realized Laura's shoulders were shaking. She was crying quietly, tears invisible in the darkness, but felt in the weight against him. He bent and kissed the outline of her hair. "What's the matter, babe?"

"Oh, it's nothing." Her voice was fragile, uncertain. "I was just thinking - more than anything, I want this train ride to end and for us to be together as a family." She lingered on the word family, then her voice hardened as though she'd pulled herself back from some dangerous hope. "But I know that's impossible. We have to ride this through. Until the end."

Tim rubbed her shoulder, resting his chin on her head. "I'm afraid you might be right," he whispered, the rhythm of the train lulling them with its deceptive gentleness.

They sat in silence again, sharing the same unspoken thought: *if there was a future for them, for Rose, it began and ended here, on this endless ride, on this damnable train.*

When Rose finished eating, Laura tucked herself back in and held the baby out. "You can burp her if you want to hold her."

Tim's heart leapt. He took Rose as if she were the most fragile treasure in existence, his hands trembling as though he held a priceless vase. "My God," he breathed, overwhelmed. "I can't believe how beautiful she is." He patted her back in awkward rhythm, imitating confidence he didn't feel. "I never... never knew a baby could change a person like this. She's peace and love and joy all wrapped into one." His voice cracked, breaking into a whisper. "I just never knew."

Laura's eyes softened. "I understand completely. I only wish we'd had the chance to share those nine months with her. I missed watching her grow inside me, feeling her kick, seeing the ultrasounds..."

"Getting the morning sickness," Tim teased, a crooked grin flashing across his face.

Laura chuckled, shaking her head. "Well, I wouldn't go so far as to say that." At that moment, Rose gave a tiny burp that startled both of them into laughter.

"You did it," Laura said with some excitement, reaching for the child. "I'll take her back if you want."

"No, I... Tim began, but stopped, startled...

A hush fell over the train. It wasn't silence, but something deeper, as if everything around them, the train, the rails, the train-car, held its collective breath. Without warning, a soft, warm glow pressed in around them, and both Tim and Laura stiffened at the same moment. Rose's tiny body grew warmer against Tim's chest, and suddenly, impossibly, both he and Laura saw it all, not with their eyes, but with their hearts.

A rush of images poured through them like light through water – there but diluted somehow: Rose taking her first steps on a sunlit living room floor; Rose laughing as she splashed in a bathtub, bubbles in her curls; Rose wobbling toward Tim holding a wooden block; Rose asleep on Laura's chest on their favorite rocker, a Golden Book laying open on the table next to them while it stormed outside in the dark; Rose chasing a butterfly in a backyard they never had but suddenly remembered as if they'd lived there for years.

It wasn't a dream, and it wasn't a memory. It was a gift, a tapestry of moments they had never been granted, stitched together as though someone, somewhere, had mercy on them.

Laura's hand flew to her mouth. Tim's breath hitched. And just like that, the glow faded, leaving the two of them trembling, holding the echo of a life they'd never gotten to live... but somehow had just lived anyway.

Tim began to speak, but when he looked at Rose, she was no longer a baby. She had grown in an instant, now a toddler in the dim glow of the train car. Another milestone had passed in the flicker of a heartbeat.

Tim stared, his heart sinking. "I think..."

"That was... beautiful," Laura interrupted his thought.

"I think things are moving along faster than we anticipated." He turned her toward Laura, whose eyes were once again wet with tears.

"Oh, Tim," she cried out, her voice frightened. "When do we get to enjoy it?" Laura's voice cracked with longing. A tear fell from her eye. "Aren't there any stops along the way to smell the flowers?"

"I'm not sure there are many flowers on this ride..." Tim began, but the words dissolved as the air thickened. Once again, shadows poured into the car, a tide of dark souls pressing in. He clutched Rose tight, shielding her eyes. Panic clawed at his chest as Laura's fingers dug into his arm.

"He's coming," she whispered, and Tim's glance confirmed the dread.

"Shh. I'll take care of it if he does."

There was no stopping the flood of despair. The car filled to bursting with the wretched, battered souls; those who had ended their lives in fear, now bound to this train. When the last of the spaces were filled, the air shifted, and the man in white appeared. A few horrified gasps filled the car, and he smiled at them.

He started at the front of the train this time, whispering into ears, dismissing soul after soul with a flick of his wrist. The procession was merciless, each moment dragging like hours, until finally he stood before them. He leaned toward Rose.

"Well, well, well! What do we have here?" His smile was saccharine, his voice spun sugar, hiding the venom behind it. "A newcomer! How precious! Now we have a whole family of interlopers!" He clapped his hands to mock them. "We haven't had a baby here in..." Mockingly, he feigned thinking, his hands to his lips. "Ever!"

Tim lunged to block him from coming near Rose, but his limbs refused him. The man in white was stopping him without even making the effort. His hand brushed Rose's curls, lingering - teasing.

"Oh, Timmy," He looked at Tim and then at Laura. "Laura... such a sweet child. And she's welcome here, of course. After all, she's your byproduct. She's not here on her own." He shrugged and gave a slight tilt of his head. "At least not yet. She doesn't even know what it means to board this train."

"Leave us the hell alone," Tim growled, straining forward. "I won't let you touch her."

The man's eyes flickered red, holding out his hands as if inviting Tim to approach him. "How's that working out for you, Timmy?"

The man in white furrowed his brows, the mockery melting into something sharper, colder. His smile widened just enough to make Tim's stomach twist. His voice was velvet over broken glass, sweet and cutting at the same time.

Tim's muscles strained against the invisible barrier that held him back. He twisted, tried to lunge, anything to close the small gap between himself and his daughter. Desperation turned his movements frantic, and every attempt felt like flailing in quicksand.

"Why don't you just save your strength?" the man continued, his presence filling the air like smoke. His voice remained calm and taunting. "Didn't I tell you before, Timmy? This is *my* train. You two were nothing but interlopers the moment you stepped on board, and nothing you do will ever change that." His smile widened, but his eyes were pitiless black. "I am in total control. Of the train. Of you. Of everything you will become."

Tim's chest heaved. The words cut, but he refused to yield. Still clutching Rose, he slumped back against the seat, trembling with helpless rage. The man in white finally released her hair, and Tim was released from his invisible grasp. He instantly pulled Rose against him, shielding her with his entire body as though his arms could form an unbreakable wall.

The man in white stepped away, not with retreat but with the casual arrogance of one who knows he cannot be defied. As he moved through the car again, he brushed past a new group of restless souls, dismissing them with a flick of his wrist. His voice, however, carried back as though he were still beside them, taunting, needling.

"Ever since I found you on my train, I've been in control of every move you've made, Lovebirds. Did you think that wedding was your own choice? Did you believe in that little fairytale you call 'meant-to-be'?" He spat the words with syrupy disdain. "Don't be silly. I put that all together. I put you in that chapel. And this..." he gestured vaguely as another soul vanished into nothing, "this child you cling to so tightly... well, maybe she's your handiwork, your ceremonial consummation, but don't flatter yourselves. You wouldn't even be here if I hadn't allowed it."

Another soul disappeared, and another, until the car grew emptier, save for the heavy presence of his voice that grew more and more menacing. "You're on *my* ride, until the very bitter end. And believe me... it will be a bitter end."

Laura clutched Tim's arm with such force that her nails dug crescents into his skin. Tim's jaw tightened, anger surging up like a tide, threatening to drown his fear. His eyes darkened, but his voice came out steady, almost defiant.

"I don't believe a word of it," he growled in defiance. "Not one damn word. You're not in control of us. You're not in control of anything." He leaned forward, glaring through the veil of shadow. "This..." he snapped his fingers, "*is* our 'meant-to-be.' And there's not a thing you can do about it. NOT A DAMNED THING!"

The man in white whipped around, his entire body stiffening with rage. His face twisted, eyes blazing red now like burning coals. The sweetness drained away, leaving only something monstrous and raw. He charged back down the aisle toward Tim, stopping two seats before them.

"You'd better watch your step, Timmy boy." His voice cracked the air like a whip. "I could dispatch you from this train right now.

I could bury you in a level of hell so deep that Dante himself would run out of words to describe it."

The threat was a spear meant to pierce straight through, but Tim didn't flinch. He leaned forward, his voice low at first, gravel grinding in his throat, then rising, louder, harder, until it thundered through the car. He gently handed Rose to Laura, stood, and thrust out his chest. He put his arms out to his sides, inviting the threat. "So? What are you waiting for? If that's your end game, then do it!"

Laura gasped, clutching Rose tight, but Tim didn't stop. He slid his body forward, subtly angling himself between them and the man. His whole frame shook with rage, but his eyes were unyielding.

That was when a small, steady voice broke through the storm, instantly calming the tumult.

"Daddy? Who is that man?"

Tim froze. His defenses crumbled in an instant as he turned. There, sitting upright in the seat, was Rose, but not the baby he'd cradled minutes ago. Not even the toddler who had just appeared. Now she looked to be about three, her curls catching what little light filtered through, her wide eyes filled with innocence and trust.

Tim's throat constricted. For a heartbeat, the world tilted. His daughter was growing before his eyes, impossibly, impossibly fast. Yet she was still his little girl. His beautiful, irreplaceable Rose.

He forced a smile, fighting past the confusion. He stepped back and touched her chin gently, tilting her face toward him. "He's no one, honey. He won't... he *can't*... hurt you. Daddy's here. Daddy will always protect you."

But as the words left his lips, Tim looked up, and the anger in the eyes of the man in white had faded into an unsettling, almost disarming blue. With a simple gesture to his left, without touching, Tim felt himself shoved to the right once more, separated from his daughter by an invisible force.

The man slithered to the seat in front of them and leaned down, those too-bright eyes locking on Rose. His voice turned almost tender. "Well, hello, young lady. My, how you've grown. And so... quickly. Pretty soon you'll be a young lady, learning all about the hardships and pains of life..."

The words dripped with a twisted kind of affection, and though his voice was gentle, the sound of it cut Tim's soul like a blade.

The invisible barrier shifted, loosening just enough, and Tim surged forward, shoving his way back between them. He planted himself firmly in front of Rose, shielding her with his body. "Why don't you go now?" he snapped at the man in white, forcing calm into his tone though rage burned in his chest. He nodded toward the front of the car. "You've got more... *customers* waiting. You don't want to keep them waiting."

The man's eyes flickered, blue fading back into bottomless black, the false tenderness vanishing as quickly as it had appeared. He straightened, towering over Tim, and backed away slowly. His hands began to flick through the shadows again, dismissing soul after soul with abrupt, angry gestures. Each vanished with a hiss of despair, and the sound scraped against Laura's nerves until she moved in to cling tighter to Rose.

At the front of the car, he turned, his face smooth once more, though his smile was venom. "Such a beautiful child you have. Such a shame..."

And then he was gone, snuffed out of existence as if he had never been there.

The silence that followed was deafening.

Tim turned immediately, his arms wrapping protectively around Rose, who was pressed against Laura's side. Both parents froze when she spoke again, her voice no longer that of a three-year-old.

"Mom, you're crushing me."

Tim and Laura exchanged a stunned look. Slowly, they pulled back, and their hearts lurched as they saw what had happened.

Rose was no longer three. She looked to be around seven, her limbs too long to be cradled, her features sharper, more defined. She wore a yellow dress patterned with roses.

Laura swallowed hard, forcing a smile that trembled at the edges. Reluctantly, she let Rose slide down onto the seat beside her. "I'm... sorry, honey." She looked up. "Tim? When does it stop?"

Rose smoothed her dress, her eyes wide with innocent curiosity. "Who was that man, Mommy?"

Laura's composure faltered. She turned from Tim, who didn't have time to reply, and fear coiled in her chest like a snake. She managed to answer, her voice unsteady. "He's... no one, Rose. Just forget about him."

Tim leaned down, ruffling her hair with a gentleness that masked his pounding heart. "Don't worry about him, sweetheart. Mommy and Daddy will always be here to protect you. Okay?"

Rose looked up at them, her expression filled with complete trust. "Okay." She smiled, the simple, unshaken smile of a child who still believes every word her parents say.

The train squealed suddenly, the sound echoing through the car. Light spilled in from the windows and the flickering lamps overhead, washing away the gloom. Rose stirred excitedly in her seat.

"Are we home now?" she asked as the train slowed to a grinding stop.

Tim stood and peered out the window, but the view offered no answers. A landscape unfamiliar, shrouded in pale haze, stretched beyond. "No," he said, his voice steady but uncertain. "I'm afraid this isn't home. But let's check it out together and see what it might be, okay?"

He reached down, taking Rose's hand. It felt impossibly strange; still small, still fragile, yet larger than it had been only moments ago. The paradox twisted his heart, but he held on tightly as they made their way down the aisle.

"Coming, Mommy?" Rose called back, her voice sweet and eager.

"I'm right behind you," Laura replied, rising from her seat. She followed, though her eyes kept darting to the shadows at the edges of the car, as if expecting the man in white to appear again.

Together, they walked toward the open door. Rose glanced up at Tim, her eyes sparkling with sudden mischief. "Hey, Dad, how do trains eat?"

Tim gasped, blinked, then turned to Laura with wide, proud eyes. She was already smiling knowingly, bracing herself, quickening her pace to join them. He stopped, crouched, matched Rose's height, his heart aching at the innocence in her voice. He wiped at the quick tears that were forming. "I don't know, honey. How do trains eat?"

"They chew chew."

The laughter burst out of Tim before he could stop it, rich and unguarded. He scooped her into his arms, holding her close, and Laura groaned, rolling her eyes, but soon her own laughter joined theirs.

"Great. Now there are two of you," she teased, shaking her head at them both.

Tim rose again, Rose's hand secure in his own. Laura stepped beside them, slipping her fingers through her daughter's. For a moment, their little family felt whole, untouchable.

"Well, sweet little girl," Laura said softly, "let's go see what the future holds for us."

Her eyes met Tim's, filled with something fragile and aching. "Missing it, Tim. We are just... missing it."

He kissed the top of her head, whispering against her hair. "Maybe now. But someday. Someday down the road..."

Laura's gaze lingered on him, searching, hoping. Her head tilted toward his chest. "I hope you're right. More than anything, I hope you're right."

And together, hand in hand, the Wentz family stepped off the train and into the next chapter.

Part Two

Sweet Rose's Suite

CHAPTER 10

G olden Field

The smell of late summer slipping into early fall floated in the air as Tim and Laura stepped off the train together, Rose lingering just behind. The shift of seasons seemed to hang tangibly around them, as if the world itself was pausing just for them. The sun burned high at its zenith, draping everything in a golden warmth that shimmered over the landscape.

The light felt almost merciful after the jolt and rattle of the train, and the frightening visit from the man in white. It was as if the day itself had been waiting for them to arrive, to give them some reprieve.

Around them, a wide field stretched outward, its grass trimmed to a soft carpet of green, framed by trees locked in the slow beauty of surrender. Leaves curled and browned at the edges, yet still clung stubbornly to branches, blazing with streaks of yellow, orange, and red. The air carried a crisp edge, sharp, invigorating, and beneath it lay the earthy undertone of fading summer. That unmistakable scent of change drifted like a promise: things beginning and ending all at once, something Tim and Laura understood all too well. The whole place felt curated, almost reverent, like a memory trying to become real, but... just out of reach.

Laura inhaled deeply, closing her eyes for just a moment. The cool, clean air seemed to settle her bones, sweeping away the disgust of the train - and for an instant, she let herself believe they were simply a family arriving at a soccer game. But only for an instant. Memory returned like a tide. With it, the image of the man in white.

"I hate being on that train," she murmured, leaning into Tim. "That man in white scares the living hell out of me." The words, soft as they were, carried a weight that seemed to dim the sunlight a shade.

Tim flinched at the words, instinctively turning and reaching to shield Rose's ears, only to pause when he realized she wasn't there. When he saw her, a few feet away, his chest tightened. Rose had grown again. What was she now? Ten?

She stood in a soccer uniform, her jersey bearing the word *Bears* beneath a cartoon bear that looked more cuddly than fierce. Shin guards hugged her legs, and her ponytail swished with every bounce as she took off running. His mind stuttered over the math - how long had passed between heartbeats - then surrendered, because this was their life now.

She waved with a broad grin. "Bye, Mom and Dad!" That grin lit him up from the inside, the way only your own child can.

And just like that, she was gone. She dashed toward a cluster of kids, disappearing into their own tiny orbit. The small world of cones and whistles and giggles swallowed her whole, and Tim felt the familiar ache of pride and fear take equal seats in his chest.

"Soccer?" Laura blinked, trying to reconcile the sudden leap in time. Her voice hovered somewhere between delight and dread, and she shuddered softly with anxiety.

Tim shrugged - helpless. "You understand as much as I do." He tried to play it off with a crooked smile, but it didn't reach his eyes. His anxiety was a match for Laura's, though neither one would admit it.

Laura's voice dropped into thought. "Maybe less. I don't know - is she showing traits we had as kids? I played some soccer in school, but I wasn't great. Sports weren't really my thing. Mostly art and... well, drugs." The confession slid out raw. "That's what I used to escape my foster parents. All of them." Her gaze drifted beyond the field as if one of those houses from her past might suddenly claw its way out of the trees and reclaim her. Anything seemed possible here.

Tim's brows lifted, half in surprise, half in concern. He squeezed her hand, just once. Not a question. Just a presence.

Laura chuckled lightly, catching his fingers. "Don't worry. I made it through." The laugh tried to erase any further concern he might have.

They walked together across the manicured grass. The field beneath their feet was too perfect, too ordered; like someone had arranged it all for them. Tim couldn't shake the sense that each step was pre-drawn, laid out the way a coach lines cones on the pitch: turn here, now here.

Ahead, a neat row of parents sat in bright folding chairs, water bottles at their feet, eyes drifting toward Laura and Tim with subtle curiosity. The silent judgment of unspoken comparisons thickened the air. Both Tim and Laura shared the same thought at once. "Are these people all..." Tim's breath caught as his face twisted. Neither one finished the sentence. They didn't have to. The veneer of what seemed normal here only made it stranger.

She motioned toward a particular family: mom, dad, and their much younger daughter, each dressed in identical tan slacks, green shirts, and glaring orange ski vests. The vests clashed absurdly with the Rattlesnakes' uniforms and the weather. Even their smiles looked ironed.

"We could have been more ready," Laura whispered, trying to break the heaviness. "I mean, we don't even have matching ski vests." Humor was the quickest out she could think of, and she felt proud to have joined in the jokes with Tim and Rose.

Tim smirked, leaning close. "Ski vests in the fall? What the..." Then, louder than he should have, "We'll be ready next time, honey! Matching ski vests for all the kids!" He raised a fist in mock triumph, and a few parents, *dead or alive,* Tim thought uneasily, turned to stare.

Laura groaned, tugging his arm. "Shh. You're always so sure there's going to be a next time. Why do you want to invite trouble from… you-know-who?" Her words hung as brittle as dry leaves, but then her face softened and she patted his arm. "Well… at least today looks like it's going to be fun. So we should embrace it, right?" She was making a promise to herself as much as to him.

"Right," Tim said, though doubt still crept around the edges of his voice. He hated how small it sounded.

Laura's eyes glistened with fierce tenderness as she turned toward the field. "Our daughter is growing up, Tim. So fast I can barely breathe. It's not normal. There's no time for bonding, for growing together, for learning what each of us is all about. What are her likes, her dislikes? What…"

"I know," Tim interrupted, looking at her as if she held the answers. "Time is elusive here."

On the field, the teams were lining up. Rose bounced on her heels, concentration etched across her face. Laura's heart swelled as she caught the little furrow in her daughter's brow, the one she'd seen in her own mirror.

"I know we haven't had much time together, but that," Laura whispered, fire flickering in her tone as she pointed toward her daughter, "is what keeps me going. That's why I'm not letting that demon in white take this from us. If this is our meant-to-be, I'm going to fight for it with everything I have. I'll hold onto it for as long as I can." Her vow was laced with hatred.

"It's the promise," Tim spoke softly as Laura looked up at him in amazement. "It's the promise that if… when… we make it through…"

Laura's amazement slid into a smile, and she interrupted, her words laced with honor. "You are my warrior, Tim." She said it like a truth she dared the world to challenge, and she looked up at him with a proud smile on her face. "I'm proud of the way you protected us on the train." Reaching up, she kissed his cheek and rested her head against his shoulder, anchoring them both.

Tim let the *warrior* title sit on his chest like armor he didn't yet know how to wear. "I was just doing what I needed…"

A breeze swept the field then, interrupting him, but carrying a faint whisper of something beneath it. Like a warning tucked inside a perfect day. A voice startled them from behind, interrupting Tim. It carried a strange clarity, as if it had been waiting for the exact space between heartbeats.

"You know, most kids who play youth soccer don't really grasp the rules. They just run around, have fun, and burn off energy. It's only the parents who like to think it's something more. Like their children are professional athletes in the making, born with talent that transcends the ages." Casual words. But they tugged at invisible threads.

Tim spun. A man stood behind them, his presence commanding without force. Shoulder-length blonde hair caught the sunlight; his eyes were piercingly blue. Something in the angle of his jaw, or the way he stood with his hands loosely at his sides, tugged at Tim like a faint déjà vu - the memory of a memory.

The man crouched beside them. His tone was calm, but each word felt weighted. "Sure, there are always a few standouts. Even the worst teams have a star." He gestured at a boy breaking free, ball at his feet. "But most of the time, it's a social game. For the kids, not the parents." His eyes flicked to a pair of fathers screaming at the referee. Then, with a glance toward Rose: "Take your daughter, for example." The way he said *your daughter* made Tim's skin buzz. How did he know...?

Tim and Laura stiffened. For once, they agreed without a word.

"Now, Rose... she seems to have a good grasp of the game." Her name in his mouth landed on Tim and Laura like both a blessing and a trespass.

Tim's mouth went dry. "How do you know her name?" The words fell sharper than he intended, more plea than challenge. But before he could demand more, the crowd erupted. All eyes swung to the field.

Rose streaked down the grass, dribbling the ball past defenders with uncanny ease. Her movements were instinctive, fluid. She took two shots, blocked, but powerful, the rebound just as fierce as the first attempt. Each miss only lit her determination brighter.

"Where did she get that?" Laura whispered, awe and disbelief tangling together with pride.

The man's presence seemed to fade, their daughter's spark pulling all of their attention away from him. For a moment, pride swelled too brightly to leave room for questions. Even the sun seemed to climb higher, the day turning brighter.

"We have a beautiful daughter," Laura murmured, eyes shining wet.

Tim puffed up. "Darn straight we do." He didn't even notice how hard his fists had clenched with pride.

Laura smiled and kissed him quickly. "Look at you, my proud warrior." Now he wore the title like a new suit, the kind any man would be proud to wear; tailor-made and form-fitting.

By the third period, the Rattlesnakes held a five-goal lead, but Rose refused to yield. She wasn't about to be shut out. An errant pass slid to her feet, and she surged forward, the field stretching before her like a stage. Only the goalie remained, crouched and ready.

"Go, Rose! Come on, honey! You can do it!" Tim shouted, voice breaking on *can*.

She twisted, struck, and the ball sailed true. The goalie lunged the wrong way. The net rippled.

Rose fell with a soft thud that initially went unnoticed.

"That's our girl!" Tim and Laura shouted, clapping wildly. Applause rang through the field.

But Rose didn't rise. Silence rearranged the day, allowing fear to reappear. Laughter and peace? Gone like a fall breeze.

Laura's laughter cracked and died. She looked in all directions, expecting the worst, expecting to see the man in white standing there with a smug glance in their direction. "Tim... is this something from him? Is this the man in..." Laura stopped mid-sentence.

Tim saw her throat tighten, the way she swallowed the name instead of saying it.

Time slowed. Tim's legs began to move before his mind caught up, his instincts thrusting him forward. Soon, he was sprinting, his face now twisted in fear. "I don't know!" His thoughts were all over the place. Run now, think later.

Somewhere in his mind, he could hear Laura's footsteps near his, but at the same time, he could feel the train's phantom sway tug beneath his feet. The man in white flickered in his mind, and Tim shoved him back. Rose lay crumpled on the grass, teammates forming a worried circle.

"I don't think she's okay," one child whispered as Tim arrived. The words pierced sharply because they were small and frightened. Tim knelt beside Rose. Her face was pale, twisted in pain.

Laura dropped beside them with something that was a combination stumble and slide.

"It's my leg, Mommy," Rose whimpered. "Something's wrong with my leg."

Laura brushed back her hair, voice trembling with forced calm. "You probably just tripped, honey. These things happen." She wore her hope on her sleeve as if begging it to be true.

"Did I score the goal?" Rose whispered, lips quivering, pain shadowing her face.

Tim and Laura laughed softly, their hearts breaking.

"Yes," Tim said, stroking her hair. "You scored the goal. You were amazing." The texture of her hair under his palm carved itself into him. He could feel his heartache forming. He turned, low and urgent: "How do we get her to a doctor, Laura? Not on the train. That monster will be waiting. There has to be another way."

Like the years that passed before them on the train, announcing Rose's growth, time felt slippery again. The world flipped like a page turning: green to white, sun to fluorescence, cheers to distant beeps from monitors tucked away unseen. It seemed to speed up to an uncatchable pace.

Tim scooped Rose up, clutching her to his chest, and at that moment, everything gave way. Grass hardened to tile, trees dissolved into white walls, parents melted into nurses, ski vests transformed into smocks. The smell flipped from cut grass to antiseptic in one jagged breath. Before he could take one step, a receptionist looked up from the counter, smiling warmly.

"Welcome to Saint Elizabeth's Pediatric Hospital. May I help you?"

For once, there was no man in white, no nightmares, just white walls and the hum of fluorescent lights.

Tim blinked hard. He fumbled for words. "Hi. Um... my daughter hurt her leg. We don't know if it's broken or just a sprain..." The word *'um'* bothered him. Lack of confidence. Not a warrior at all.

"Certainly," she said, sliding a clipboard toward him. "You'll need to stay and fill out these forms. Your wife can take her to triage." She nodded in Laura's direction.

Laura muttered, taking Rose into her arms the best she could. "How are you going to fill that out, Tim? We don't *have* a history."

"I'll make something up," Tim whispered, grabbing the pen and looking at the clipboard. His hands shook. He prayed his lies would be believable and legible.

When he looked up, Laura and Rose were gone. His heart lurched. No time for sitting comfortably, he put the clipboard against the wall and wrote. Then he wrote faster. Time, elusive, slipped by all around him and he recognized it. It made his anxiety flourish.

When he returned the clipboard minutes later, the receptionist nodded. "You can go back to triage now." She set the papers aside, and they vanished.

Tim blinked, shook his head, and bolted for the room. Time was very slippery now. He had to find a way to catch it. As he ran, he spoke – forever Tim – humoring no one but himself. "Well, at least now I know how to fill out paperwork in the afterlife. And that it doesn't matter."

The turns to triage were minimal, and when he reached Laura and Rose, Rose's head was resting against Laura's shoulder, exhaustion fogging her face.

"You okay, honey?" Tim asked softly, brushing her hair and breathing heavily from his frenzied pace.

"My leg hurts, Daddy. But I'm okay." She tried to smile, but it was a fragile thing, and it pierced Tim's heart.

"As soon as the doctor sees you, he'll take care of it."

"Okay," she whispered.

On cue, a nurse appeared in the doorway. "Wentz?"

Tim lifted Rose carefully, as if she might vanish between steps, and they followed the nurse to Exam Room 3.

A young doctor appeared moments later. "Hi, I'm Doctor Joe," he smiled as he shook hands and set his chart on a table at the side of the room. "What happened, Rose?"

"I was playing soccer," she whispered. "I tripped. My leg hurts, and I'm tired. I want to sleep."

He pressed along her shin. She yelped. Laura flinched like the pain had jumped from Rose into her.

"Okay," Dr. Joe said gently. "We'll need an X-ray."

"Is it going to hurt?" Rose asked, voice trembling.

Laura smoothed her hair with a smile. "No, honey. It's just a picture." She tried to sound comforting, but wasn't sure she was pulling it off.

Rose nodded bravely as the nurse returned with the wheelchair. Tim set her in the chair, and they wheeled her away, leaving Tim and Laura a moment to look at each other in disbelief.

It was a short-lived moment, however, as time bent again - twenty minutes vanishing in the blink of an eye, not leaving Tim and Laura any time to linger on their fears. The nurse returned with Rose.

"It's still happening," Tim spoke softly to Laura. "Nothing moves at the speed it's supposed to here. The pages of our story are flipping before we even get a chance to read them." His voice was filled with panic and anger combined.

When he returned to the room, Dr. Joe put the scans on the light box and glanced at them. "There's a break, I'm afraid, but it's not bad. The tiredness is probably from the trauma. You'll need a cast, Rose. Soccer season's over, I'm afraid."

Tears pooled in Rose's eyes. "But, I love soccer," she choked out.

Laura hugged her in a motherly manner that somehow seemed embedded in her, even though she didn't understand how. "I know, honey. You can play again next year. I promise." Her promise hung like a lantern in a tunnel – small, struggling to be hopeful, but still there.

Not to be excluded, Dr. Joe immediately got to work on the cast, the materials appearing before him as if he were a strange magician conjuring them from somewhere unseen. With steady hands, he wrapped her leg. Getting up from his chair, he washed his hands in the sink and crossed the room to a box sitting in the corner unnoticed. He reached in and returned with a stuffed giraffe. "Here. This should make you smile."

Rose clutched it tightly, smiling as he had promised. "Oh! I love him. I'll take him everywhere. I'll call him Doctor... Doctor Joeraff!"

"Oh, I love it," Dr. Joe replied, leaning down and giving Rose a hug. "You be careful now, okay?"

"Okay," Rose smiled as she hugged the giraffe.

Tim and Laura both thanked him, and Tim lifted Rose once more. He gave a sigh that was both relief and concern, and began carrying her back to what he thought would be the lobby. They hadn't taken three steps from the room when they were outside.

An empty lot loomed in front of them. Laura paused, scanning the dark lot that could have been for parking... or waiting, she couldn't tell which. Her voice seemed to grow distant with thought. "Nothing. No discharge instructions, no signatures. Just like you said. Another page turn." Laura turned toward Tim. Do you think this is where the train is?"

Tim closed his eyes, picturing the man in white. His stomach turned, and he shrugged. "I don't know. I wish I did, but..."

The sky darkened. Parking lot lights buzzed to life, and Laura touched his arm. "C'mon, warrior. Let's go look, shall we?"

Behind them, Rose's small voice grew, tired but steady. "Daddy, where are we going?"

Tim, not sure he could fill the new role that Laura had thrust upon him, stared into the night, shadows stretching farther than they should.

He swallowed hard, hiding the fear rising in his throat. "We'll figure it out," he whispered – more to convince *himself* than Rose.

A cold wind slithered through the lot, and somewhere in the distance - not close, but not far enough - something metallic shifted, like wheels settling onto a track.

INTERLUDE I

T he Hallway

The hospital was too bright. Too clean. Too normal.
Tim stepped into the hall anyway, leaving Laura and Rose behind. He told himself he was just grabbing coffee, but really, he needed air. Space. A moment to breathe. To slow down and try to rein in this time speeding away from him.

His fingers brushed the coins in his pocket - change from their trip to the beach. That seemed like years ago. He fed them into the vending machine and watched the cup drop, listened as bitter liquid hissed into it. He wrapped his hands around the warmth, but it didn't reach him.

Something was wrong.

The air. The walls. The light. All of it was slightly off, like a photograph tinted on his phone with one of those cool filters - interesting, but not... right.

The floor didn't feel solid anymore; it felt fragile, as if it might give beneath his shoes. The hallway stretched, receding even as he stood still, cup in hand. Voices at the nurse's station dulled, as if the world were being muted one dial at a time.

Then, he saw him and he froze.

At the far end of the corridor, a man appeared. Not a nurse. Not a doctor. He walked with calm certainty, shoulder-length blonde hair catching a strange golden light bleeding into the hall, surrounding him, making him seem almost angelic... The light gathered to him like water filling a sudden void.

Tim's chest seized. "You again." His voice cracked.

"Yes," the man said evenly, lifting his hands slightly. "Me again."

"Stop following us." Tim's words came sharper than he intended. He braced for the echo, but the hall swallowed the words whole.

"I'm not following you, Tim," the man replied calmly. "I was sent." He said Tim's name like he'd been there the day it was chosen, like he'd known him forever.

Tim barked a laugh. "Sent? By who?"

The man chuckled softly. "Technically, Tim, it's whom in that instance."

Tim stared. Grammar? Now? But before he could respond, the lights flickered. The hospital peeled away. Outside the windows, no streets, no cars, just fields drenched in amber glow. A rush of hay and earth filled his nose.

Tim blinked hard, his heart pounding. "What's... what's happening?"

"This place," the man said softly, looking around, "is unraveling. Growing thinner by the hour. You've already felt it, the sway of the train, the way one world shifts into another. Time racing. None of it's fixed, Tim, and it's pulling you somewhere. Somewhere you and your family may not want to go."

Tim shook his head, backing away. "You don't know us."

"I know enough." The man's eyes burned steadily. "Parents fear many things. But the greatest is this: letting your heart walk around outside your body. That's the weight you carry every time you look at Rose."

Tim swallowed hard. The words had landed too cleanly.

"You're not here by accident," the man pressed. "You and Laura left Earth on your own accord, but you were placed on this train for a reason. Maybe salvation, who knows? But this salvation comes at a cost. Trials are being set before you. Not to break you, but to forge you. This train, this journey, it's toward that salvation. But you'll need strength to finish it. Courage. Because just like on Earth, the one in white..." His eyes darkened. "...he already thinks you're his. And no matter what love and joy you cling to here, he won't stop until you surrender."

Tim's throat constricted. "So, what? You're saying all this - everything with Rose, Laura, the hospitals, it's just a test?"

"Yes. Each step of the journey is another test." No apology. The man's gaze held him, unblinking. "You don't have to believe me. Not yet. But you will. And when you do, you'll know, you'll have to stand - if you want to survive."

The golden haze collapsed. Linoleum, fluorescents, and nurses laughing at their station returned. Tim stood frozen, his coffee cooling in his hand. The man was gone.

The title that Laura had given him, Warrior, rang briefly in his ears until - from down the hall, Rose's voice floated out: "Daddy? Were you just talking to the angel?"

Tim's knees nearly buckled. His eyes snapped open.

He was never there.

They were on the train.

The seat pressed into his spine as if it had never let him go, and when he looked at Rose, she was smiling up at him. "Were you, Daddy? Were you talking to the angel?

Tim opened his mouth to speak, but the squeal of brakes tore through the air, and the world lurched toward the next stop.

CHAPTER 11

A ngel's Trail

"What on Earth is going on?" Tim muttered.

The train screeched to a stop, and the doors abruptly opened - faster than they usually did. From sheer habit, Tim and Laura both started to stand, and Laura fell back to her seat. The last she knew, she had been holding Rose, the ten-year-old Rose, comforting her as they rode in silence - but now, it wasn't Rose's voice as they knew it, but older, sharper, dripping with teenage sarcasm.

"Mom, why are you holding me? Put me down." Laura heard the disgust in her daughter's voice and was taken aback.

Laura shook her head to steady herself. She started to answer, concern already rising along with the embarrassment in her cheeks. "Because I don't want your leg to be..." But as she looked at her daughter, her voice faded. Rose was no longer in a cast. She looked older now, maybe thirteen. The shift hit Laura like a cold wave along the shore - not violent, but unavoidable. Every time the train stopped, reality seemed to reorder itself a little more boldly, as if it no longer cared about easing them in.

"Honey," Laura breathed, bewildered. "What happened to your..." She turned, wide-eyed. "Tim, are you seeing this?"

Tim nodded slowly, not paying attention to Laura or Rose following behind him, but easing toward the train door, hardly eager to take in their new challenge, but moving forward swiftly as if on offense.

As they exited the train, however, Tim started to move with hesitation. Everything in his dream showed this place thinning, unraveling – yet *this* stop looked just as solid as it could.

When he exited, he stood in a sun-drenched field bordered by gentle woods. Nearby, a stable bustled with activity as people prepared for trail rides. Beautiful horses of all sizes and colors stood in a neat row, saddled and waiting.

"Horses!" Rose shouted, already sprinting toward them.

"Honey, watch your..." Tim started, but Laura touched his arm.

"Her leg is healed," she said softly. "I tried to tell you. And she's no longer that ten-year-old ball of sweetness. Now she's a teenager. God help us, Tim," she murmured.

Tim chuckled in disbelief and held out his hands in resignation. "I don't think we have anything to do with it, honey. We have to make the best of each situation. We take each step as it comes. We have to pass each test."

Laura shot him a questioning glance. "Test?"

Tim shook his head as if he had said the wrong thing. A word that should've meant something simple suddenly felt loaded. Anything could be a test here. Everything could have consequences.

"Hey," he took her arm, walking forward, changing the subject. "I like horses. You?"

"Only if they're not too fancy," Laura shrugged. "Nice redirect, by the way."

Tim shrugged and blushed. He let a breath in and out to evade Laura further. "If you like horses, then I suggest a trail ride."

When they arrived at the stable, Tim paid the stable hand with the money that never seemed to lessen, and soon the three of them were being matched with horses. The guide asked each of them about their riding experience.

"Trail rides only," Tim said. "Nothing wild."

"Same," Laura added.

"Never," Rose chimed in, her face filled with nervous excitement. She was bouncing on the balls of her feet. It looked as if she were ready to jump out of her skin; she was so ready to begin. Even as a teenager, she was excited, but Laura remembered *her* teenage years, when everything could change like the flip of a coin.

The guide paired Rose with a mild-mannered horse named Astro and gave her a helmet. Tim and Laura reluctantly put on theirs. Safety helmets... here? In this place? Tim shook his head in disbelief. "Oh well," he mused. "Safety first." Rose giggled.

As they mounted their horses, Tim glanced at his daughter, his teenage daughter. She was beautiful and strong - growing fast. The kind of child you hope to see every day for the rest of your life.

Deep down, he hoped that this would be their life now, but did he really want this existence, travelling from location to location to see what new test or turmoil the man in white had arranged?

Then, there was the blonde-haired man in his dreams. That man unnerved him, mostly because he didn't understand him. There was something suspicious about him. It wasn't danger he sensed - not exactly. It was more like recognition without memory, a familiarity that had no rightful place in Tim's life. He couldn't quite place...

Needing to get the subject out of his head, Tim trotted over to Rose. "Hey, kiddo, remember when you broke your leg playing soccer?"

"Barely," she replied, dripping with exaggerated disgust. "I was, like, ten. Oh my gosh, Dad, why would you *even* bring that up?"

Tim laughed, raising his hand in defense. "Dad, question. Sorry. Just making sure you don't plan to do it again today."

"Don't worry," she scoffed like a disgusted teenager. "I'm not going to break my leg *riding a horse*. I'm not even using my legs." Rose started away, steering Astro like an expert.

"Unbelievable," he murmured as she left.

From the corner of his eye, Tim sensed a presence. Another horse had joined their group. In the saddle sat the man with shoulder-length blonde hair that was covered by a riding helmet. The man from his dream.

He smiled at Tim and nodded at Rose. "She seems ready."

Tim blinked. "What the..." He wanted to ask about the dream. He wanted to ask about the thinning reality and the salvation, and the tests. He wanted to ask about it all, but he also wanted to be as composed as possible with Rose around, so he shut his mouth. He cleared his throat. "Yes, she is. First time, I think. At least *I've* never taken her before."

"She'll love it," the man replied with a wide grin. "First rides are always special. As long as you're careful." The man turned toward Tim and gave him a soft sort of glare. His final words lingered, unmistakably ominous. It was as if he already knew the outcome of the ride, the way someone knows how a story ends before the first page turns.

Tim stared after him for a few seconds longer than he had liked, then turned to check on Rose. "I'd... I'd better catch up," he said, but the man just nodded, somehow knowing - a knowledge that Tim didn't care for.

Laura trotted up behind Tim, and the blonde-haired man fell in line behind her. Tim sighed at her comfortable presence, grateful that the short passage with Rose and the blonde-haired man was over.

Still, a mild uneasiness crept over Tim; bad things happened when the blonde-haired man was around. He was there at Rose's soccer match, and she broke her leg. He was in Tim's dream just last night, and he told him all sorts of things he didn't care to hear. It occurred to him that these events had all happened within a short 24-hour time frame, and he remembered what the man had said, This was a test. But was it a test Tim was willing to take?

He had the sudden urge to drop out of line and go visit with the blonde-haired man to question him further, but the trail guide barked out orders as if she knew his intentions.

"Remember to keep your horse behind the one in front of you. If it wanders off the trail, gently pull on the reins and right it."

Tim stayed put, tension coiling beneath his ribcage.

They entered the woods. The trail narrowed, the trees thickened, and Tim felt the closeness of it all pressing around him.

Every sound - the hooves, the rustling branches, even Rose's laughter - felt slightly delayed, like reality was being re-broadcast a fraction of a second behind itself. It was just like everything else on this trip: the train, the broken arm, the man in white, the blonde-haired man. It all threatened to close in on him.

It's only woods, he reassured himself as he took a deep breath. *They've done this before.*

"She looks like a natural," the blonde-haired man said, his words aimed at both Tim and Laura,

Laura glanced back and smiled. "She really does. I didn't know she had that in her."

"Gets it from her father," Tim chimed in, turning his head back the best he could, trying to saddle the fear in his thoughts.

"Oh, I don't know about all that," Laura teased.

They shared a laugh as Rose rode confidently ahead.

Eventually, the terrain shifted to a rocky path. The guide slowed. "Easy now. Let them step slowly. They've been here before - you haven't."

Tim relayed the message to Laura. "Careful over the rocks – slow steps."

Rose spoke gently to Astro, rubbing his neck to steady him. "It's okay, boy. Just some rocks. You can do it."

The horse responded calmly, stepping over the stones with care.

Following the rocky terrain, they all sighed in relief when they reached a creek. Here, the guide called for a short break so the horses could drink. Tim led his horse beside Rose's and smiled at her. He was so glad to be by her side again. The connection between them was real, despite her teenage hormones. "Having fun, honey?"

"Yes, Daddy. Thank you. I love Astro. Thank you for bringing me here."

Tim nodded. He had no more to do with this than any other part of the trip they had taken so far, but he didn't want to get into that with Rose. "You're welcome. I heard you talking to your horse," Tim smiled. "I think mine is named Maverick. Mommy's is Cinder."

"Like Cinderella," Rose giggled. "Maverick, Cinder, and Astro. Cute."

She looked toward Laura, who was talking to the blonde-haired man, and concern flickered across her face. "Who's that man Mommy's talking to?"

Tim followed her gaze. "I'm not sure, honey. He was at the soccer game too. Said you looked like a natural." Tim gave Rose a proud smile, not realizing just how out of context that comment might be to her.

Rose scrunched her brow. She wasn't buying his fatherly attempt at flattery. She was clearly focused elsewhere. "The soccer game when I broke my leg? That's kinda weird, doncha think?" She shook her head. "Seems kinda creepy, following us. Still... I think he looks like an angel. Do you think he looks like an angel, Daddy?"

Tim raised a brow. The word 'angel' twisted oddly in Tim's stomach. In any normal world, it might've been sweet. In this one, it felt like a warning disguised as innocence. He remembered her words from the train just before arriving here - *Were you talking to the angel?* The memory made him choke on his reply. "Hmm... an angel, you say? Well, I don't know about that. I think he's just a guy..."

Thankfully, the guide called them back in line just in time. As they re-formed, two riders slipped between Laura and Tim, putting some distance between them and making Tim uncomfortable, as if uncomfortable were something new.

"Where's Mommy?" Rose asked, twisting in her saddle.

"Behind us, sweetheart. Some other riders and their horses got between us; that's all. It's okay."

Rose nodded, smiled, turned her attention forward, and they continued. "Ready, Dad? Let's go." She gave him a gesture forward with her head and started, her teenage angst thankfully on hold for now.

Only about a mile after watering the horses, the peace was shattered.

Without warning, the horse ahead of Rose reared hard, letting out a sharp whinny. A snake had slithered across the trail, and the horse reared up, causing the other horses to panic as well. Someone who had seen the slithering serpent screamed, "Snake!" and added more fuel to the panic.

Rose pulled back on Astro's reins, trying to steer him away, but it was too late. Astro panicked right along with her, spinning sideways.

The frightened horse directly in front of them kicked out wildly. Its back leg struck Rose squarely, knocking her from Astro's saddle, and Tim screamed, scrambling down off of Maverick. "Stop! Stop the ride!" Tim bellowed, his voice cracking with terror.

The guide in the back galloped quickly after Astro, who was beginning to wander, and grabbed his reins.

"Whoa!" others echoed, pulling their horses to a halt.

Tim hit the ground running and sprinted to his daughter. This wasn't just fear; it was the sickening déjà vu of loss replaying itself. The universe kept dangling Rose in front of him, then yanking her away. Horrible visions flashed through his head, visions of the man in white, but Laura's arrival shattered them. She was still on her horse, reins in her hand, and the power of unity with Tim in her voice.

"Are you okay, Rose?" they asked in unison.

No response.

From behind, the blonde-haired man trotted up, concern on his face, "Is she okay?"

Tim quickly shot him a glaring glance because he knew that the answer was already somewhere out there in the cosmos, and he probably didn't want to hear it. "We'll handle it."

The man nodded, his expression softening. "You got it, Tim." He led his horse away from the frightened family.

"Rose? Honey?" Tim knelt beside her and whispered to her, his voice filled with a mix of sympathy and fear. She stirred, slowly, her face in a grimace.

"Hi, Daddy..." she mumbled, dazed. "Why am I on the ground?"

"You had a little trouble with your horse," he replied. "Did you hit your head?"

"I'm not sure. My arm hurts, though. A lot." She began to cry gently. "Did I break another bone?" she asked with almost certainty before chuckling. "I told you I wasn't going to break my leg."

Her sobs deepened, and Tim looked up at Laura, shaking his head. His eyes had gone wide with fear. "We have trouble again," he murmured, hoping that she would hear him.

She nodded grimly, muttering under her breath – a string of curse words Tim presumed were targeted at the man in white. She sighed in resignation. "We'll get her to the hospital," Laura said firmly, already bracing herself.

"Do you think Doctor Joe will be there, Mommy?" Rose whispered, drifting in and out of consciousness – somehow catching every word.

"I'm going to guess he most certainly will," Tim rubbed her head and tried to ease her mind.

Once more, he recalled the blonde-haired man's words as he scooped Rose into his arms, and Laura guided her horse beside. *This place is unraveling. Growing thinner by the hour.* Just how thin, and how long would it last, Tim wondered.

Without either one of them noticing, the blonde-haired man followed quietly behind.

At the forest's edge, the world melted away. It didn't feel like a smooth transition this time. More like a tear, as if the woods had been ripped aside and the hospital shoved in place. Neither structure was meant to exist where it suddenly did.

A different receptionist smiled at them, but Tim recognized her as one of the trail guides they had seen just moments before. The words, *"This place is unraveling,"* struck home with him again, but this time he understood that there were only so many players in this skit, and their roles shifted. "Can I help you?" she asked as if reciting a familiar script.

"Us again," Tim said tightly. "I think Rose may have a broken arm this time," Tim said, shaking his head in disbelief. Broken leg, broken arm. Part of him hated how practiced he sounded. It was as if this sort of thing were becoming routine. What else was there? He shook the question away because he didn't want the answer.

As if she had memorized lines in this otherworldly play, the receptionist expertly spoke with a rehearsed smile pasted on her face, "Have you been here before?"

Tim paused, then nodded, trying to keep his urgency and his growing frustration at bay. "Yes. Wentz."

"Ah, Rose," the receptionist replied kindly, absently typing into the keyboard in front of her. "That's right. Go ahead to triage. Doctor Joe will be with you shortly."

"Doctor Joe!" Rose briefly stirred, then lay her head back down on Tim's shoulder. Even her excitement looked thinner now. It seemed as if it was stretched over exhaustion that didn't belong in a kid her age. She spoke so beautifully that Tim thought maybe she was an angel herself.

"Daddy... why is that angel still following us?" Rose murmured.

Tim turned with anger swelling in his chest, and saw the blonde-haired man standing in the corner - helmet gone, perfect golden hair loose around his shoulders.

"Why *are* you here?" Tim asked, voice low and gravelly. He wanted to make it clear that the man/angel's presence there was no longer welcome.

The blonde-haired man held out his hands in a gentle, open gesture. "Just checking on Rose. That fall was pretty rough."

"She'll be okay," Tim said firmly. He studied the blonde-haired man more closely with squinted eyes. "How did you even get in here?"

"I walked through the door, same as you, Tim. Is that a problem?" The man spoke calmly. "I care about her. And you."

"I don't want you following us anymore," Tim said, stepping closer and tightening his hold on Rose. His voice shook, not with anger, but with a parent's terror. Whatever this man was, he felt too close to the center of their unraveling. "From now on, following us isn't possible."

The man's blue eyes darkened with what could only be termed sadness. "I'm just looking after Rose... and you and Laura, Tim." He shifted his feet, then, in a calm voice, spoke as if changing the subject. "You know, they say being a parent is like letting your heart walk around outside your body."

Tim turned. "That's what you said in my drea..." A nurse interrupted him, calling his name, and he turned toward her. Remembering the blonde-haired man, Tim turned back to get in the last word, but he was gone.

"Mister Wentz?" The nurse repeated gently, and Tim shifted his attention once more toward her, regaining his focus as well. "Room three."

Room 3 again. Another barely-there wait, no time at all, as if time wasn't very stringent here. Then, Dr. Joe entered.

"Hey, there, folks. Looks like it's been a few years."

"Oh, I don't know," Tim muttered, rolling his eyes. "Feels like this morning, if you ask me."

Rose woke the best she could, offering a tired smile. "Doctor Joe! I remember you! You gave me a giraffe."

"Rose, right?" he asked, returning her smile.

"Yes!"

"So what happened?"

She quickly relayed the story about the horse, the snake, and the fall.

"Pain level?" Dr. Joe asked, running his hand expertly over Rose's arm.

"Seven or eight," Rose replied. "But I'm tired. I just want to sleep."

Dr. Joe looked at her, concerned. "You were tired last time, too, if I remember correctly. Let's get an X-ray again."

Right on cue, a nurse entered the room with a wheelchair, and Tim set Rose in the seat. As she took Rose away, Tim suddenly realized that Laura had been there the entire time. How had he missed her, and how did Dr. Joe and Rose speak as if it had really been years when in fact it had only been days? A day between each incident – maybe.

"Hey..." he called to Laura, but she followed Rose without any reply, and Tim had no choice but to start after them. Dr. Joe touched Tim's arm to stop him.

"Stay a moment, Mister Wentz. I want to run some tests - just to be sure. She's tired a lot."

Tim hesitated, then nodded, his concern now heightened. Was there something else going on besides a broken arm? His heart sank. "What does that mean?" But Dr. Joe was gone. Tim raised his hands in disbelief.

Exhausted himself, Tim dropped into a chair near the bed, closed his eyes - and for the first time in a long while - slept soundly.

Finally, time behaved itself.

"Tim." A hand on his shoulder woke him. Dr. Joe had returned. Tim looked around, but Laura must have remained outside the room.

"Well, it's a break - we all suspected that. We'll cast it. But I'd like to follow up on those tests. We'll get back in touch with the results." He gave Tim's shoulder a light squeeze and his best attempt at a smile. "It's routine, Tim. Nothing to worry about. Just routine."

Tim nodded without saying a word, but the worry was lapping around the edges of whatever this place was. Nothing here was ever routine, and his chest was beginning to compress in on itself.

A fog continued to grow in his mind as Rose and Laura returned to the room and Dr. Joe worked gently, wrapping Rose's arm from the kit that once again magically appeared before him.

When he finished, he walked over to the box in the corner and returned with a soft stuffed horse. He smiled as he handed it to Rose. "Since you love horses, Rose, here you go. This one's a much safer ride."

"Thank you!" Rose beamed. "He can be friends with my giraffe!" She stood and hugged Dr. Joe, and he returned the embrace, her exhaustion evident.

Dr. Joe smiled. "Well, you're all set, Rose. Take care."

"Thank you, Doctor Joe."

Dr. Joe patted Tim on the back and whispered so Rose couldn't hear him. "I'll let you know what I find... if there's anything."

Tim nodded, anxiety growing with each passing step. If it was routine, as Dr. Joe had repeated, why did he keep bringing it up? Routine wasn't a word that belonged here. Not when the world kept bending itself around them like a story trying to skip to the ending.

Outside the room, Laura greeted Tim and Rose. She immediately picked up on his expression.

"What is it? You look like you've seen a ghost."

Tim shook his head. "Hopefully nothing." He kissed her on the head. "Where have you been? I haven't seen you for... it seems like ages."

Laura placed her hand on Tim's back and gave him a strange look of confusion. "I've been here all along, sweetheart. You sure you're okay?"

Tim stared at her in disbelief and amazement. "I... I'm not sure anymore. This place is changing. It was *never* normal, but now even the not-normal isn't normal," he spoke as they continued to pass through the waiting room.

At the exit, the doors opened with a soft *whoosh*.

As she crossed the threshold, Rose tripped, catching herself on the doorframe with her good arm.

"Careful," Laura said with a laugh. "Let's not break any more bones today."

"Sorry, Mom." She laughed, and Laura brushed her hair with her hand. "It's okay," she smiled.

But Tim's mind spun with worry. The hospital doors felt less like an exit and more like the beginning of another turn in a maze - one where the walls kept shifting faster than he could make sense of them.

As they stepped out into the familiar parking lot of the hospital, a place they knew should be a field for riding horses or a field for playing soccer, Rose looked up at Laura.

"Where are we going now, Mommy?"

Laura glanced up and met Tim's eyes.

"That... is a very good question." And the worst part was, Tim realized, he wasn't sure he wanted to know the answer anymore.

INTERLUDE II

The Waiting Room

Tim realized that he was pacing the waiting room, his hands shoved deep in his pockets. His legs couldn't keep still. Laura was back with Rose while the nurses worked, and he couldn't stand sitting in another plastic chair pretending like everything was normal.

He glanced at the monitors on the wall over the nurses' station and saw that they had writing on them, but it was writing that didn't make any sense. The letters were all jumbled except for one set: Patient - Wentz, Rose.

The chairs were the same blue as every waiting room he'd ever hated; his reflection, where he could see it in the monitor glass, looked like a man mid-fall. Similar to the way he felt.

Nothing was normal here. "Everything is getting thinner," the blonde-haired man said, the one Rose had called the angel. The memory rubbed him like sand at the beach. No matter how much he tried, he couldn't eradicate it. He began to hyperventilate as he got to his feet, panicky. He bent at the waist, his hands on his knees, but then began to ease up when it occurred to him that this was probably just the dream again.

He looked around, his heavy breaths subsiding. Recognition snapped into place; the air tasted faintly of metal. The lights weren't consistent; they fluctuated bright and dim over and over again. It all felt eerily like before.

He had to be on the train. Asleep again.

Still, a vending machine hummed in the corner. A TV on the wall by the vending machine played muted cartoons, bright colors flickering across the space. Cartoons that made no sense. Men with dragon heads, children with dog heads, women with daisy heads.

He turned.

A family, it had to have been a fake family, sat across the room, whispering to one another as though this place and these... these actors could actually be trusted.

The fluorescent lights, amid their dimming and glowing, buzzed like tired bees; the clock made a noise that pretended to be ticking.

Tim couldn't shake it. The air again. Too thin. Too fragile. He picked up the pace of his steps and felt like he could punch a hole into the drywall and leave a dent in reality.

Frantic and filled with growing anxiety, Tim turned toward the hallway. He wanted to go back and get Rose and Laura... Laura. Was Laura even still here, or was she on the train where he must be? Thinning. All thinning.

The hall stretched before him, and Tim gasped. The blonde man was suddenly leaning against the wall like he'd been waiting there all along. Same shoulder-length hair, same piercing blue eyes. The light collected on him as if directed there, refusing to move away, like a spotlight from the mezzanine above.

Tim's chest burned. "You have got to be kidding me. You brought me here again." Anger came easier than fear, and he latched on to it. He spun around and then back again. "I knew it, this time. I smelled the train. And... the lights fading and glowing..."

The man straightened, arms loose at his sides. He offered up a snide smile. "Ah, you're catching on, Tim. You're figuring things out. And the reason we're here again? It's because you needed to see me." The man dropped his air of posturing and put a hand to his chest. He smiled. "Name's Perniel, by the way..."

The name fit him the way mountains fit a horizon - inevitable once you saw it, or in this case, heard it. "Perniel, Peniel, Phanuel. All variations on the Angel of repentance and hope."

"No, no, "Tim shot back, his voice sharp. "I don't need you. What I need is for my daughter not to keep getting broken. What I need is for my wife not to keep watching it happen. And what I need most is for you to stay out of our lives."

Each need landed like a fist on the table of the world, but appeared to do nothing to Perniel. Instead, they vanished into the air like they'd been swallowed whole. Perniel stepped closer, his eyes narrowing. The room's edges furred and wavered with each of his steps.

"You think this is just about broken bones?" His voice carried more weight now, not loud, but heavy enough to make Tim's skin prickle. "You think these trials are about casts and doctors and trips to the hospital? No. They're about you, Tim. You."

The you *pinned him to reality more effectively than any hand could, and Tim winced and wanted to get away, but his body had already decided to believe, even if his mind hadn't.*

"Every fall, every fracture, every tear in your daughter's eyes, it is sharpening the blade inside you," Perniel said, his words deliberate. "Because whether you want to face it or not, you are standing between your family and something darker than broken bones. You are their defender..." He let the words echo in the hallway. "You are their protector."

A picture flashed before Tim, him, small, with a shield too big for his arms, and he hated how true it felt. Still, he tried to deny it. He shook his head and took a step back. "No! You talk like you know everything. But you don't. You don't know me. You don't know Laura. And you sure don't know Rose."

Perniel's jaw tightened. For the first time, the calm shimmer of the blonde-haired man cracked. "You're wrong, Tim." The crack let light through.

Tim froze, and suddenly he could feel the floor; he could remember the sway of the train as Perniel approached him.

"I know her name. I know her spirit. I know what she was meant for. And I know the enemy that hunts her is not a stranger in white. It is the oldest liar in existence. He already thinks you've given up. He already believes you're his. Have you ever heard of Phanuel, Tim? Old angel, good at getting rid of the accusers who try to stand before God to accuse others on earth?"

Tim's throat constricted. He wanted to yell, to shove the man away, but no sound came. Silence pressed a hand over his mouth.

Perniel leaned in, his voice low, sharp enough to cut. "I didn't expect you to have. Well, he was my father, Tim. And because I loved my father as much as you loved yours, I agreed to intercede in your case."

The word father detonated softly inside of Tim, and his eyes narrowed. Recognition filled his eyes. "Wait. I saw you at the wedding. You talked with my dad. He..." Memory shifted, revealing an angle he hadn't seen.

"That's right. Your father. He searched. He scoured the cosmos. He conquered. And he pleaded with my father to help you, Tim. He knew where you were heading after his passing, and he needed to intercede. He's your warrior." Perniel waited, but Tim could only stare. The angel continued. "Now, the man in white? He's one of the accusers. His main goal is to run that suicide train, to bring judgment to those who try and - well, you get my drift. But he's not going to get to you. Not if I can stop him."

The phrase suicide train rang like a hammer on steel, and Tim could feel the swaying of the vehicle again. He writhed at the reminder of why he was there.

"But I don't understand... I don't understand how any of this... I don't understand why... Rose. Why, Rose?"

Perniel's anger rose. "You do understand, Tim. If you do not rise, if you do not step into what you're called to be, then you will lose her. And not just her body. Her soul."

The syllables found the exact place his fear slept and dragged it into the light. Tim's breath came ragged, and tears began to flow. "Laura? Rose? Both?" He placed his hands to his eyes. "Stop!" The tears embarrassed him; they also told the truth.

"I won't," Perniel said, almost fierce now. "You've wasted too much time running, doubting, pretending you can't carry this weight. But Laura sees it. Rose sees it. Even she calls me angel while you scoff. And I will tell you the truth, whether you want it or not." His eyes flared with a light that made Tim look away.

"Like your father before you, you are their warrior. Just like Laura told you. But it's up to Laura. It's not up to Rose. It's up to you. And if you keep refusing to see it, then you will hand them over without even realizing it."

The word warrior settled on his shoulders like a mantle that might be armor or a burden, or maybe both.

Tim clenched his fists, tears stinging his eyes. "I don't know how to believe this!"

Perniel's voice lowered again, calm returning but edged with iron. "This is no longer about whether you believe me, Tim. It's about whether you're willing to fight. It's about whether you are willing to be the husband and the father that Laura and Rose need you to be." He let the words sink in briefly, then continued, albeit a bit softer now. "Because the man in white is patient, Tim -and he's waiting for you to do nothing." Perniel waited for Tim to reply, then cut the air one last time. "And do you know the man in white's name, Tim? He has one of the oldest names in history. He is Apollyon. The destroyer." Perniel stared down Tim one last time. "If you don't fight? He will destroy you and everything you have."

Tim stared at Perniel as he vanished. The room flickered. The golden haze returned for a breath, then snapped away. TV sounds filled the silence again. Nurses laughed behind the counter.
Normalcy returned, slightly crooked.

Tim blinked, then realized his heart was pounding. He looked around, but it was true, Perniel was gone.

The train's brakes squealed, and Tim woke, gasping with fright this time.

Next stop.

Those two words felt like a verdict.

From the darkness, Rose's small voice drifted, weak but steady: "Daddy... the angel says you're not ready yet."

Tim reached out and pulled Rose closer. He closed his eyes and waited for the door to open and the journey to continue mercilessly.

When the light pierced the darkness, he braced himself; not for the landing, but for the letting go it might require. Not ready yet?

Tim tried to thrust out his chest and stepped forward, but he wasn't sure it was enough.

CHAPTER 12

Prescription: Love

There was a collective sigh as Laura and Rose joined Tim in standing for their next stop. The train and its persistence were beginning to wear on all of them.

When they stepped outside, they quickly realized they were moving faster than a walk. It took a few seconds to register - they weren't walking at all, they were on bicycles, gliding effortlessly down a paved trail that wound through sun-dappled trees. None of them took the time to think about how this was even possible, going from walking to biking, because nothing here surprised them anymore.

The wind hummed in their ears, cool and alive, and the rhythmic click of pedals blended with the rustle of leaves. It was like the horse trail had been reborn - only smoother, cleaner, and impossibly bright.

"Hey, Mom! Check this out!" Rose laughed as she pedaled ahead, her voice ringing like a bell through the trees. She was older again - sixteen, maybe - and she rode with an easy confidence that made Tim's heart ache. Once again, he had missed it all; *they* had missed it all, years 1-16. And, once again, the break in her arm was gone. Gone, but not forgotten. The memory loomed like an omen that couldn't be dismissed.

Laura and Tim exchanged glances, half shock, half delight, then burst into laughter as they tried to keep up. They had no recourse but to take it all in. This was the moment they were afforded. And if the danger of Rose having another accident lingered out there somewhere? Well, it would have to wait. They were blissful in their circle of laughter. For now.

It had been years since either of them had ridden a bike. The movement was awkward at first, but soon their bodies remembered, and the air filled with their laughter; the simple, perfect kind that happens when life briefly forgets all of the pain and heartbreak it can produce.

"Wait up!" Tim called, his lungs already protesting. "You have younger legs! And better lungs! No fair!"

He wheezed but laughed through it, his face flushed. For that brief stretch of road, everything shimmered with joy. The waiting room, Perniel, and Apollyon were not here. Wherever they were, he was sure they would return. For now, however, he shook the thought away and glanced back at Laura, his perfect, perfect, Laura.

"Don't look back at me, you dork!" Laura shouted at him beneath laughter. "You're going to crash!"

Tim grinned at her and then nearly did, swerving wildly before catching his balance again. "Whoa. That was close."

"Listen to Mom, Dad!" Rose almost sang with joy, her hair streaming behind her as she called upward to the air, hoping to catch the wind that would carry the words to her parents. She pedaled harder, and it seemed as if the awkwardness of her beginning teen years had faded, replaced by the experience of learning how to cope.

Their laughter was infectious, but it was also short-lived. None of them saw Perniel appear beside Laura until his shadow merged with hers on the asphalt.

She glanced to her left and let out a sigh. "Oh crap. You're back." She looked forward once again, her tone edged. "That can't be good news."

"Why not?" he asked lightly, pedaling beside her. "Can't I just enjoy a nice bike ride?"

"Some people might buy that," Laura said flatly. "But not me. I've got you figured out."

"Do you?" His smile was small, unreadable as he pedaled into the sunshine. "Go on, then."

"You're something... celestial," she said, searching hard for the word. "Not quite angel. Not quite devil. Here to protect us? Maybe. Or maybe just to watch."

He tilted his head, amused. "You're pretty observant, Laura."

And with that, he pulled ahead, his golden hair catching the sun.

"So which is it?" Laura called after him. "Angel or devil?"

She shook her head as he offered no answer.

Up the trail, Perniel matched pace with Tim.

"Back again?" Tim said, trying to disguise his anger. "You know, you shook me last night. Are we really in that much trouble?"

Perniel's shrug was a quiet ripple of movement. "What do you mean?"

"Don't play coy," Tim said, breath uneven. "You keep showing up. At every twist. Every fall. Every night in my dreams. You give me these dire warnings about this reality thinning, fading away. You tell me I have to step up, I have to be the protector. That's not a coincidence."

"What if it is?" Perniel replied, his tone full of love and kindness. He gave a backward shrug toward Laura. "What if I'm just here to observe, as Laura said?"

Tim barked a laugh, the wheels of his bike giving a slight wobble. "There's no way that's true. Coincidence doesn't work that hard. This *place* doesn't work that way. This place - despite being beautiful at times - is evil. I know it. I can feel it. And the fact that you told me about... him, Apollyon, last night... I can only deduce that the moment of judgment is close by. I don't want it to be, but I'm almost certain that it is." Tim's voice faded at the end of his speech, and he fought off tears as he hoped Perniel would move on further.

Perniel's mouth curved, that half-smile that never reached his eyes. "Not now, Tim," Perniel said softly. "Down the road, maybe. For now, enjoy the day." His eyes betrayed him for just a flash, but flash enough for Tim to take notice and for his heart to ache. There was so much more in his words. So much more unspoken.

Perniel pedaled away and seemed to vanish around a corner.

Tim slowed, watching Perniel fade. He continued the slower pace until Laura caught up to him again. He nodded in Perniel's direction. "So what do you think?" he asked. "Is Perniel an angel? Protector? Or is he something else?"

Laura smiled at him, and Rose circled back to them from somewhere unseen. They all stopped pedaling, and Laura dropped her voice to keep the conversation between her and Tim. "That's his name? How do you know that?"

Tim shrugged. "He told me." He wanted to tell her more, so much more, but Perniel had told him that *he* was the one who had to be the protector, and no matter what that looked like, he had to do it. If he hadn't been doing it before, he would start now. And, if he hadn't been doing it enough, he would step it up.

"Interesting," she said, lowering an eye at Tim. "Well, he's something, that's for sure. He always shows up when something bad happens. I used to think he was a warning sign. But maybe... maybe he's our shield. Maybe he's the one holding back the man in white."

Tim was glad to see her understanding, and he felt a bit relieved that he wasn't holding the entire bag himself. "You think we're in danger?" Tim asked, testing Laura's premonition. "More than we thought?"

"Yes," Laura said, coldly. "And I think it's getting worse."

Tim's voice softened. "But we have hope. We have each other."

Laura looked up at Tim with coldness in her eyes. "Is that enough, Tim? Is it?"

She climbed back on her bike and started pedaling.

Tim looked over at Rose, who was giving him a half-smile, and then nodded and started pedaling again. "Angel, Daddy."

There had been no reply to Rose's words - Tim couldn't think fast enough to offer up anything remotely intelligent. Instead, he kept pedaling on, watching Laura and Rose move on further and further away from him.

It's getting thinner by the moment.

Tim was still trying to take in all that was happening, and he didn't have time to notice Rose when she stopped next to Perniel quite a distance ahead of them.

Thinner.

Rose squeezed her brakes when she pulled up next to Perniel.

"Hey, Rose," the angel greeted her arrival.

In her awkward, flirty, teenage voice, Rose returned the greeting. "You're too handsome not to be an angel," she teased.

He smiled faintly. "Teenagers." He shook his head. "Why do you think I'm an angel?"

"I just... sense it," she said. "Something about you feels protective."

He didn't answer. He didn't have to. Then, as if he knew what was coming next, he looked closely at Rose as she continued.

"I know I'm sick," she said quietly, looking around uneasily. "I feel it. I don't know how long I have, but I know it's not forever. Every year passes in minutes, and I try to pretend they don't. Every day is another three years." She looked back at Perniel, tears beginning to form. "My broken bones heal overnight, my casts are removed while I sleep on that... that fuc... ugh, that train. I hate it. I want to have a normal life so badly, but it's not gonna happen." She started to cry, but then looked away. "I don't think my mom and dad know yet. But they will, won't they?"

Perniel's eyes softened. "Your dad, he knows... some things, but not..." He placed his hand on her shoulder and sighed. Rose turned back toward him. "Yes, Rose. They will."

"How long?" she whispered.

"I can't say. This world isn't real. It's just a glimpse. A may-be. I can't count your time in minutes, days, or years, only in moments. Events. But I'm here for you."

"Minutes?" Rose's eyes clouded with tears. "Minutes?" She sobbed some more, as silently as possible. "You're an angel," she said, starting to pedal away. "So, please be there for me."

Perniel smiled but said nothing as she moved on by herself.

Just the fact that Perniel had stopped and talked to all three of them was ominous enough. When they finally caught up to each other and realized that he was gone, it was as if the joy that had been there before his appearance had been run over by the train that they had come to hate so much.

They didn't speak; they just pedaled and looked at the scenery, taking in the beauty that surrounded them, always beauty in this thinning, fragile world. In this place, in this world where the walls were getting thinner, and the weight of their existence was getting heavier, they moved on as if waiting for the next shoe to fall.

And it fell.

Rose's handlebars wobbled. Her front tire jerked from side to side. "Oh no!" She screamed a horrible scream, as if everyone already knew and felt what was happening. She called out in dread, "Dad," and the sickening scrape of rubber and aluminum filled the air before the crash.

Perniel was there beside Rose in a heartbeat, appearing from somewhere unseen, his bike now nonexistent. Tim and Laura were seconds behind, and Tim pushed past Perniel without a word because no words needed to be spoken. *He* was the protector.

Tim scooped Rose up, his adrenaline rising. "Rose! Are you okay?"

Her eyes fluttered as once more the tired state began to reappear. This time seemed to be worse than any time before. "Daddy... I'm not sure I can move anymore."

Panic cracked open inside of Tim as Laura turned to Perniel, her voice breaking with anger and fright. "I thought you were here to help, Perniel! Do something!"

"It's not my place," he said as he stood, his voice quiet, sad, and firm.

"Then get the hell away from us!" Tim roared at him, struggling to hold on to Rose. Clutching his daughter, he ran in no particular direction, calling out something that anywhere else would make no sense. "I need the hospital! I need Doctor Joe! Show me the hospital!"

The air shimmered. Doors appeared.

They stepped through.

Inside, the nurse smiled like she'd been waiting forever. "Mr. Wentz. We've been expecting you. Doctor Joe will see you now."

They were in chairs.

Dr. Joe sat across from them, his voice gentle but grave.

Tim and Laura looked around, confused, but expectant that something like this would happen.

"This is it, isn't it?" Tim asked out loud, pulling Rose closer to his chest, not wanting to release any of what he had gained: his wife, his child, his... life.

But as if Dr. Joe were the messenger of fate himself – and maybe he was – he spoke words that would force the air out of both Tim and Laura's lungs.

"I'm sorry, but Rose has multiple sclerosis. MS. It affects the brain and spinal cord."

He explained the rest: the frayed myelin, the scrambled signals, the slow betrayal of the body, but Tim and Laura only heard bits and pieces. The initial shock was enough.

"I get blurry vision sometimes," Rose said as she held as tightly as she could to Tim. "I thought it was just because I was tired."

Joe nodded. "Fatigue is common. So is weakness, balance issues, even memory loss."

"But my life hasn't been that long," Rose murmured. "I don't remember much." She managed to look at Dr. Joe with sad eyes. "I know you know." She looked around, her voice rising with anger. "I know you all know. All of you... You angels or whatever you are. You're all in on it, and I'm your puppet..." Rose buried her face in Tim's shoulder and began to cry.

Tim and Laura exchanged a helpless glance. How could they convince her this wasn't life in the normal sense? How could they tell her that they would fight for her in this life and the next if they could, when *they* didn't even know if it was possible?

Tim changed the subject, shooting for a target of hope. "What are our options?"

"There's no cure," Joe said softly, glancing at Rose. "But there's management. Relief."

"Then we'll do that," Tim said. "Whatever she needs."

Joe hesitated, then stood. "Come with me a moment." Tim eased Rose into Laura's arms, his eyes meeting hers in hopelessness. He followed, and once they were away, Dr. Joe spoke again, his hand on Tim's arm.

"Tim, I don't understand everything," he admitted. "I know you've been here before. I know who the blonde man is. I know this isn't reality, but there is hope..."

"You know about Rose?" Tim asked.

Joe nodded. "She isn't alive. But she *is* real, somewhere, and... you love her. Isn't that enough?"

Tim wiped his face, but continued to look at Dr. Joe. "This journey gave me Laura, and then Rose, Doc. I can't lose them. They're all I have."

"Then take this," Joe said, handing him a slip of paper.

Prescription: LOVE. Take one tablet daily as needed.

"That's what I prescribe most often here," he said with a weary smile. "It won't cure Rose, but it might keep you whole when things get..."

Tim smiled weakly. "When they get impossible? When the thinness is gone, and the darkness takes over?" He looked at the prescription again and put his hand on Dr. Joe's shoulder. "We'll take it. For Laura. For Rose."

Joe returned the smile. "Most people never find what you have. They never get this far. I hope you hold onto it. Most people, the man in white just..." he shuddered at his thoughts.

Tim swallowed hard and looked at the ceiling, then back to Dr. Joe. "This prescription, is it for here or for... after?"

Dr. Joe patted Tim's hand. "Take as needed," he replied, then vanished, leaving Tim in the hallway.

He hesitated for a brief moment, then returned to where Laura was rocking Rose the best she could in a stationary chair. He showed the prescription to Rose. "This is what the doctor gave us. We'll try it. Whatever happens, Rose, we love you. We'll take as much love as we can get our hands on and..." he didn't get to finish. Rose put her hands on his arm.

"As long as I get to stay with you and Mommy," Rose said. "That's all I wish for. Even if... even if..." Her tears erased the rest.

Tim leaned in and pulled himself close. Laura turned her head away, her shoulders shaking. She seemed fragile, as if something inside of her was collapsing, as if her entire world was on the precipice of disaster.

"Mommy," Rose whispered, "it'll be okay."

Laura nodded. "I know, baby." She continued to sob.

They held each other in a family embrace, broken only by Rose's soft words. "Where's my angel?" she asked.

Tim smiled faintly. "Probably waiting outside. I was kind of mean to him. But I needed answers."

"You needed truth," she said.

He nodded. "Yes, my love. I did."

"I think I understand, Daddy." Rose continued. "This isn't real, where we are. Is it? It's just a possible future. So if I go..."

"Rose…" Tim interrupted, but she silenced him with a finger.

"If I go, Daddy, will you come back for me? In real life?"

The words nearly broke him, but Tim nodded. How did he respond to that request when he didn't understand? He took a deep breath, said a silent prayer, and tried to change fate. "I will. I promise."

"Good," Rose whispered and smiled. "I'll wait."

"We'll find you," Tim said. "No matter what."

Dr. Joe abruptly returned, holding a small bottle in his hand, and he held it out. "Love. Take as needed."

Tim shook his head. "Thanks. But I don't think we'll be needing it. We have love right here. In ample supply."

Joe tilted his head, smiling. "Well, that is better than a pill, the natural kind, but take it anyway. Just in case."

Laura started to stand with Rose in her arms, and Tim helped her to her feet. They thanked Dr. Joe and then started to leave the room.

At the door, Laura asked, "Are we ready?"

"We are," Tim said.

"Let's go see what's next," Rose beamed.

At the end of the hallway, Perniel waited for them. Watching. Smiling.

"What a beautiful family," he whispered to no one. "So full of love."

Tim raised the bottle, shook it, and grinned faintly. "Exactly what we have. Lots and lots of love."

Perniel slipped an arm around his shoulder, and together, they walked through the double doors one more time.

INTERLUDE III

The Shadowed Hall

Tim leaned against the cold wall, head in his hands. His body shook; not from fatigue, but from the fear he couldn't voice. Rose had suffered too much. Laura was fraying, and he was powerless while the world around them kept thinning, fading at the edges.

Perniel had told him he needed to be there for them, to be their warrior, but how? How could he do that when it was all so much? So heavy?

The lights above him flickered. At first, he blamed faulty wiring from this... this non-existent place. Then the air shifted, the familiar pull, the dimming of sound. The floor swayed beneath him like the train again, and he knew. Another dream.

"Not now," he muttered somewhere in the darkness, somewhere in his sleep.

But he knew. Perniel was here.

The blonde man emerged from the far end of the corridor, eyes like blue fire, stride deliberate. He no longer looked like a gentle messenger. He looked like a soldier with orders.

Tim bristled. "What now? Another riddle? Another test?"

"No riddles," Perniel said. His voice was steel now. The kindness was gone. "The time is at hand."

Tim's stomach twisted. "What does that even mean? You have so many riddles, so many unfinished statements."

Perniel stepped close, his presence pressing like heat. "It means your world is about to collapse. And you will have to take that one step, make that one choice that changes everything. I want to know if you will be ready."

Tim opened his mouth, but Perniel's voice cut through him as the angel raised his hand to cut Tim off. "Don't ask what it is. I won't tell you. Just know this: everything you love, everything you've come to hold dear, will hinge on you taking that one step."

Tim shook his head, fists trembling. "You keep saying that, take charge, be the warrior your family needs. I try! I try as hard as I can, yet nothing changes! Rose keeps getting hurt, Laura's falling apart, and I just keep... failing! Still, you come every time I sleep, and you demand more. How? You want me to fight something I can't even see?"

"Yes," Perniel said quickly and with authority. The word struck Tim like a hammer. "You think your job is to fix broken bones? It isn't. You think your strength is in carrying your daughter from one room to another? It isn't." Perniel's voice lowered to a growl. "Your strength will be tested where no doctor can reach, where no nurse will come running, where no hospital exists at all. You will face him - the man in white - and if you're not ready, you will lose more than you can bear."

Tim's knees buckled. "Stop. Don't - don't say it."

"I will say it," Perniel snapped. "Because someone has to. You want comfort here, Tim? There is none. You want guarantees? There are none. What you have is this: the chance to stand. The chance to fight. The chance to refuse surrender."

Tim's throat was raw, and he could feel the unleashing of tears. "And if I fail?"

"If you fail," Perniel said, voice low and terrible, "everything falls. Rose... Laura... You. You will get what you thought you came here for. And the man in white? Apollyon? He wins."

The words broke something inside Tim, and he sank against the wall.

Perniel's hand gripped his shoulder, firm and grounding. His voice grew a bit more reassuring. "But you are not meant to fail. That is why I am here. That is why Rose sees me for what I am. That is why I will not stop reminding you." His eyes blazed with light. "Your father didn't fail you, Tim. Don't fail Rose. Pay attention. Be ready. The hour is almost here."

A golden haze surged through the hall, filling it with fierce brilliance, then snapped away. The fluorescent buzz returned. Nurses laughed distantly. A monitor beeped.

Tim blinked. Alone again.

From somewhere next to him in the darkness of the train came Rose's small, tired voice. "Daddy... the angel says the time is close."

Tim put his head back against the seat of the train, even though he could still see the remnants of the hospital, and breathed labored breaths. His heart was pounding like it wanted out of his chest.

Did he have it in him to be just like his father and search the cosmos for the answers? Was he the warrior his father was?

Tim closed his eyes and prayed that he was.

CHAPTER 13

The Sea Between Worlds

The moment they stepped out of the hospital room, the heat of the day struck like a wall. It wasn't just warmth, it was *living heat*, rich with salt and sunlight and the hum of waves rolling somewhere close. Rose lifted her face to it, stretching out her arms as if to embrace the whole sky. She let out a long, audible sigh.

Tim blinked - and froze. It was all too much too soon.

He'd had another visitation from Perniel, but this time there was no train, only a different destination. The nightmare continued unimpeded.

Most importantly, this time, Rose wasn't a child anymore. The awkward, tender girl he'd been carrying from hospital to hospital was gone. In her place stood a young woman - nineteen, maybe, wearing a bright bikini patterned with blue and coral that would make any father want to find the nearest tourist trap and purchase a hoodie for her to wear. Her skin gleamed in the sunlight, her movements unburdened. In the real world, she'd be able to legally make her own decisions, to be on her own. That wasn't lost on Tim, nor did it make the matter better.

He opened his mouth to say something about modesty, about covering up, about being careful, but stopped himself. He remembered what had just happened in the hospital. Time was folding in on itself, and every version of her was slipping past him like waves between his fingers. This moment, this fragile, golden moment, might be all they had. She deserved to live it.

"I like your suit, Daddy," Rose said, smiling.

Tim looked down and blinked again. He wore blue swim trunks with little white seashells scattered across them. "Thank you," he said awkwardly, his cheeks pink.

Laura laughed, the sound bright and unrestrained. "Those are pretty sporty," she teased, brushing a strand of hair from her face.

Tim turned to her, and the world tilted. She wore a white bikini, a sheer cover-up fluttering against her legs. He'd seen her naked before, of course, but this was different. This was sunlight and memory and a love sharpened by loss. He realized, maybe for the first time, that loving her wasn't just comfort; it was a need. It was faith. It was survival. She truly was his meant-to-be.

Behind them, Perniel trailed in tan slacks and a yellow Hawaiian shirt, sandals sinking into the sand. He didn't belong here, and yet he did. His presence cast a thin shimmer over the world, like the light that comes before a dream fades.

No one spoke of him. Not yet.

All three, Tim, Laura, and Rose, knew it in the marrow of their bones: this might be their last day together. If not now, then soon. So they would live. Every second. And Perniel... Perniel could wait.

Hand in hand, they stepped onto the warm sand and toward the body of water that lay just out of reach.

"Where do you think we are, Dad?" Rose called out, already ahead of them.

Tim squinted at the horizon. "Well, I can tell you where we're not. This isn't Virginia Beach. It's too clean, too empty. It's like a place that hasn't decided to exist yet."

"It's still beautiful," Rose said, her eyes wide. "I can't wait to get in!"

"Do you know how to swim?" Tim asked, half-teasing, half-trying to remember some time that he had taught her. He came up empty. All there was was the train. There was no other existence.

Rose grinned. "I hope so. I think you taught me somewhere along the way." She laughed, pulled free of their hands, and ran toward the surf.

Laura frowned, her smile slipping, her eyes growing wide. "Do you think that's safe?"

Tim laughed, chasing after her. "I certainly hope so! We'll be right there with her."

Laura muttered to herself, "We can't always be there." But by the time she said it, Tim was already gone, footprints scattering behind him in the white sand. She followed to the water's edge.

The ocean was cool and vast, curling around their legs in foaming ribbons. Sunlight rippled across the waves, magnifying the colors. For a moment, it felt like they *had* returned to Virginia Beach - the air alive with laughter and salt.

Time, though, was wrong again. It didn't move forward or back; it folded in on itself. Past and present pressed together like two photographs stuck in the same frame, and Tim tried to understand, to comprehend its existence.

"We have a beautiful daughter," he said, breathless.

Laura nodded. "I'm proud of how she carries herself. How she handles... everything. One day you're a kid, the next you wake up sick. Then you open your eyes, and nineteen years are gone. I don't know how she does it."

Tim followed her gaze. Rose was splashing at something unseen - maybe memory, maybe joy. "I don't know either," he said softly. "But I'm glad she does. Whatever time we've got with her, it's bonus time now. I'll take every drop of it."

Laura smiled faintly and stepped back toward the sand to lie down, tilting her face toward the sun. Tim joined her, sinking into the warmth beside her. "I'm not ready for the water yet. You can go if you want."

Tim looked at Rose and then at Laura and decided to give Rose her freedom for however long she could have it.

That was the mistake.

While they sat and watched Rose, Laura shielded her eyes from the sun and looked up at Tim. "Do you think she knows?" she asked.

Tim nodded and exhaled deeply. "She knows."

Time just settled there, unbroken until -

It wasn't. Everything shattered in one stolen breath of peace.

The splash came first. Not the playful kind. The wrong kind. A sharp sound that sliced through laughter.

Then came the cry. Tim was up before his mind caught up, sprinting toward the surf. The sand scorched his feet, but he didn't feel it. "ROSE!" he shouted, his voice growing raw.

"Tim!" Laura screamed behind him. "What's happening?!"

He didn't answer. He couldn't. All he saw was his daughter thrashing in the water, her body jerking. A seizure. She was going under again and again, arms flailing once, twice, then gone.

No, no, no! Not like this!

He dove headlong into the surf. The water swallowed him whole, the salt burning his eyes. He clawed through waves, searching, heart hammering.

Then he felt it - a shape against his legs. He reached down and pulled her up.

"ROSE!" he gasped, dragging her to the surface. Her head lolled, hair plastered to her face. Her eyes were closed.

He turned and staggered toward shore, her weight heavy in his arms that were growing tired with each passing second. The tide fought to take her back, but Tim wouldn't let it.

On the beach, Laura was screaming her name as she arose and ran toward her daughter.

Behind her, Perniel stood perfectly still, the wind tugging at his shirt. He was watching and waiting in silence. He stood guard like a sentinel bound by rules older than time.

Tim fell to his knees in the sand, clutching Rose to his chest. "Come on, baby. Come on." He started compressions. He couldn't remember the ratio: Thirty compressions? Two breaths? What was it? Seven compressions? It didn't matter. His body just moved.

"Are you sure that's right?" Laura cried, voice shaking.

"I don't know!" Tim yelled. "I'm just - trying!"

He pressed, breathed, pressed again. Nothing. Her chest rose and fell, but she didn't stir.

Laura sobbed. "Don't let her die, Tim. Please don't let her die."

His arms burned. His chest felt like fire. The sound of the waves blurred into a roar. "You want to take over?" he gasped.

Laura didn't move, frozen in horror.

"LAURA!" he screamed, voice cracking. "TAKE OVER! I can't!"

Something in his tone snapped her out of it. She dropped beside him and took over compressions, sobbing between counts.

Perniel turned away. His eyes dimmed, reflecting nothing but the water's endless shimmer. He already knew. There would be no saving her. Not this time. Maybe in another world. Maybe after the train came again, but not here... not now.

Laura gasped and pushed until her arms gave out. Tim tried again, one last desperate time.

Then they both stopped and crumpled together beside her.

The waves lapped quietly at their knees. The world had gone eerily still.

Laura's voice broke the silence, raw and shaking. "Why, Tim? Why her? She... she was innocent in all of this. This was our ride. This was OUR DAMNED RIDE, TIM! WE DID THIS!" Laura collapsed next to her daughter.

Tim couldn't answer. He only looked toward the horizon. The sky was starting to darken - not with storm clouds, but with the slow fade of worlds colliding, folding into each other.

Somewhere beyond that veil, the man in white was smiling.

And deep inside, Tim felt the truth slide cold and sharp into his chest: the next stop was coming. It was coming soon, and it would demand everything.

INTERLUDE IV

The Last Warning

The world had gone silent.

Tim sat in the wet sand, Rose's body limp in his arms. The tide came and went, whispering over her skin as if the ocean itself were grieving. Laura knelt beside them, eyes red, her hands pressed to her mouth to keep from screaming.

"Rose," Tim whispered, brushing her hair back. The sunlight was dimming, pulling gold into gray. He rocked her gently, the way he had when she was small, when she'd wake from nightmares crying about monsters that weren't real. Except this one was.

Behind him, Perniel stood motionless at the edge of the surf, the hem of his shirt soaked and clinging. His hands were at his sides, fingers trembling. The light around him flickered like a candle about to go out.

"Do something," Laura said, her voice hollow. "You said you were here to protect us. DO SOMETHING!"

Perniel didn't answer. His jaw flexed; his throat worked, but no sound came. The wind picked up, and sand swirled around his feet.

Tim lifted his face. "Why won't you help us?" he shouted, voice breaking. "What's the point of you being here if you can't stop this?"

Finally, Perniel spoke, his voice raw, stripped of that celestial calm. "Because this isn't something I can stop."

"Then what are you?" Tim snapped, standing now, shaking with rage. "You talk about tests and trials, but you stand there and watch my daughter die! What kind of twisted test is this?"

Perniel's eyes darkened. "Do you think I don't feel it?" he said, stepping forward, his tone sharp as lightning. "Every breath that leaves her body burns through me like fire. Every tear you shed, I carry. But this, Tim - this is the turning. The moment all of it begins to collapse. I told you this was coming. I warned you, Tim. I told you to get ready." He paused and caught his breath. "Well, now it's here."

The air shimmered. The shoreline bent, warping like glass under heat. The world was growing thin again.

Tim's breath came ragged. "You said this was a test. That I was supposed to fight. I DID FIGHT! I DID!" Tim broke down crying. "So, tell me, Perniel, where's the fight in this? Where's the victory in watching her die?"

Perniel's wings flared - not seen, but felt - a pulse of invisible energy that sent the air vibrating. The ocean trembled under it. Tim and Laura looked around at their surroundings, unable to make sense of it all.

"You fought, Tim. Yes, you fought boldly, but this is not the end," he said fiercely. "It's the edge. What you choose next will decide if she stays lost - or if the path can still be redeemed."

"Choose?" Tim barked. "What choice do I have left? She's gone... Rose is... gone." Tim fell back to his knees and placed his hand on his daughter's leg.

"The path between despair and defiance," Perniel said. "Between surrender and faith. The man in white will come. He always comes when the heart is broken. And he will whisper that this was mercy. That letting go is peace. He will spout his BS that the fight is done. And then? And then, Tim and Laura, what will you choose? He'll offer you comfort in the 'yes', but it's all lies."

Tim got shakily to his feet again and wept with his hands out to his sides. "And what am I supposed to do? Punch him? Yell at him? Pray?"

"Stand," Perniel said with strong resolve. "Even when it feels like standing is impossible. Even when every part of you wants to fall."

He stepped closer. The wind howled, the horizon bending farther away. "You don't see it yet, but you are the only thing that is keeping this world from collapsing entirely. You are the thread. If you break, it all unravels. It fades to nothing. And your ride? It will all be meaningless."

Tim sank back to his knees, tears streaking his face. He looked at Rose - so still now - and shook his head. "I can't do this anymore."

"You can," Perniel said softly, kneeling down next to him. "You must."

Laura turned, her voice trembling. "Why her? She's just a child." She turned away. "I'm with Tim. I'm done." Her face went blank.

Perniel's expression cracked. "Because even heaven prays for the innocent."

The ocean thundered louder, rising higher against their legs. Lightning split the sky - not white, but gold - and the air tasted of salt and ozone.

Perniel looked around him, and his voice lifted over the storm. "The man in white is moving, Tim. Laura. The veil is nearly gone. When he comes for you, Tim - when he asks you to let her go, Laura - you will have one chance. One step. Take it, or everything ends."

Tim's body shook with sobs. "You said this wasn't the end, so why does it feel so final?"

"It isn't the end," Perniel said, his voice trembling now, equal parts fury and grief. "But it can be. The choice is yours." He looked at Laura as if begging them to stay united.

The sky flashed again. The beach flickered, and suddenly the sand beneath them wasn't sand at all - it was tile. The surf became the hum of fluorescent lights. Rose lay across a cold table, still and pale, a hospital monitor flatlining in the distance.

Laura screamed. Nurses appeared and vanished like smoke. The sound distorted, echoing in strange, hollow loops.

And then... silence.

Only Tim and Perniel remained. The angel's shoulders sagged, his face carved with exhaustion.

"This is the thinning," he said quietly. "This is what it looks like when hope starts to die."

Tim looked up at him, face streaked with tears. "Then bring her back. Give her one of Doctor Joe's Love pills. Do something!"

Perniel hesitated. "If I could."

"You can," Tim said, standing now, voice trembling. "I've seen you bend this world. You can do it again."

Perniel looked away. "There are laws even angels cannot break."

Tim stepped closer, fury shaking through him. "Then what good are you?"

The question hung between them like a blade.

"What the hell good are you?"

Perniel's jaw tightened. "I am the last wall between you and despair, Tim. I am the echo of every prayer you never said. And I will not let you give up."

He knelt beside Rose, brushed his hand through her hair, and whispered something too soft to hear. A single tear fell from his cheek onto hers. The monitor flickered once - just once - and then flatlined again.

Tim's eyes widened. "What... what did you do?"

"I reminded her of your love," Perniel said, standing. "That's all I'm allowed."

Laura gasped, clutching Rose's hand as her eyelids fluttered, then fell still again. "Do it again. You do it again!"

Perniel turned to Tim, the weight of centuries in his eyes. "I can't. She's between worlds now. One foot here, one foot beyond. If you want to bring her back, you'll have to follow her. But be warned, the man in white waits there, and he does not lose easily."

The golden light began to creep up his arms again, dissolving him at the edges.

"Perniel!" Tim shouted. "What do I do?"

"Stand," Perniel said again. "When the train comes - stand."

The last of his voice broke apart in the air, scattering like dust.

The world flashed once, and the steady rumble of train wheels returned - closer now, heavier, echoing through every heartbeat.

Tim clutched his daughter's hand, eyes on the door that was already beginning to glow.

The man in white was here. Decision time was at hand.

They stood, Rose vanishing at their feet, and they took the step. Together, yet separate, they took the step.

Part Three

Off The Rails

CHAPTER 14

The Choice

The train moved through darkness so absolute it felt alive, pressing against the glass like stale breath. Inside, the lights were dim - gray, sickly, as though even the bulbs had given up trying to shine. There was no reason for it.

Tim sat beside Laura, their knees almost touching, but their worlds miles apart. He tried to speak softly, to coax her into saying something, anything, but she only stared out the window into the darkness, her reflection lost against the void beyond. The hum of the train was the only sound between them.

Perniel sat a few rows away, his face turned toward the aisle. The sight of him there - on the train, inside this space of souls - was unsettling. He didn't belong here, and yet he looked like he carried every burden in the car. Every so often, he glanced back at Tim and Laura with an expression that hovered between pity and sorrow, as if he already knew what was coming.

Tim turned toward Laura again. Her profile was still, pale in the low light. He took a breath and tried hard to sound hopeful. "Remember when we had Rose?" His voice trembled. "That trip... it was beautiful. I keep thinking - if we ever got the chance again, wouldn't you want to? To go back, to start over, to try again?"

Laura didn't move.

"Rose was beautiful," Tim whispered. "Her curls. That laugh. The way she'd call for us, 'Mommy,' 'Daddy,' like we were her whole world."

Nothing. Not even a blink.

"You remember the soccer game?" he pressed on. "How she ran down the field, how proud we were? Or that bike ride, her curly hair flying, laughing like she didn't have a care in the world?"

Laura's lips trembled, but no sound came. Tears tracked down her cheeks, quiet and endless. She looked to the left, toward the windows. Even further away.

Tim's own vision blurred. He was about to reach for her, to try and generate some hope, when the air shifted. The temperature dropped.

At the far end of the car, the man in white appeared.

The lights flickered, the hum deepened into something that felt like a heartbeat and thunder. One by one, seats filled with dim, flickering shapes - souls. Some wept quietly; others sat with heads bowed, eyes hollow.

Perniel stood abruptly, his wings invisible but *felt*, the faint shimmer of unseen feathers in the air. His gaze locked on the man in white.

Apollyon moved with quiet certainty, his shirt impossibly white in the darkness. He seemed more confident now, more in control as he stopped beside the first of the lost and spoke to them in a voice that was smooth and cold, a voice that promised relief.

Then came the flick - a single motion of his wrist. The soul vanished.

The air rippled like heat over asphalt.

Perniel's jaw tightened. He stepped toward the back of the car, where Apollyon had not yet reached. His voice, when it came, carried a strange warmth amid the pleading and panic. "It doesn't have to end here," he told a woman whose face was bruised, wrists marked with old pain. "I know what's brought you here. But this, this is just one stop. You can still turn back. You can still choose life."

The woman looked at him blankly, eyes unfocused, and Perniel could see that hope was too far out of reach for her.

Apollyon appeared beside her in an instant. "You have a choice," he said. His voice was gentle now, deceptively kind. "Do you want to continue? To carry your pain longer? Or do you want peace?"

She stared through him for a moment, then gave a small, broken nod.

Apollyon smiled politely. His wrist flicked.

She was gone.

Perniel's voice cracked. "You erase them without a word of hope. You promise peace, but provide the opposite," he said. "Apollyon, you're an evil man."

Apollyon turned toward him, the corners of his mouth curling. "And you aren't? You promise them miracles. You tell them they'll wake up better and start again. You give them false hope, but I give them... truth." He stepped closer. "*I* do give them peace, just maybe not the peace you want. And we both offer mercy, Perniel. Mine just works faster."

"You don't know that," Perniel hissed. His light dimmed slightly, like a flame bending in the wind.

Apollyon moved to the next soul - a thin, trembling man clutching a torn photograph. "Make your choice," Apollyon said.

Perniel interceded. "It doesn't have to end this way. I can undo what you've done. Say the word."

The man's eyes lifted, hungry for release. He nodded once.

Apollyon smiled. Flicked his wrist. Gone.

He turned back toward Perniel. "You see? It's what they want. They're tired of your sermons about hope. You have nothing to give. Nothing. Just like all of the empty promises in life." His words were spoken with a serpentine hiss. "Why do you think I work here? It's much easier. Redemption? Too much work."

He moved down the aisle, the edges of his coat brushing against each seat as if claiming them. "And look at this couple," he said, gesturing toward Tim and Laura. "The interlopers. They've been here longer than most. They've tasted what might have been. They've been to multiple places, seen a myriad of 'what ifs'. I'm not sure how all of *that* happened, Perniel," his eyes flicked to Perniel, "but I'm guessing you had something to do with it."

Perniel's voice rose. "You had something to do with it, too, you evil, vile monster. You followed along every step of the way and then... then you took their daughter. You fed on their pain."

Apollyon's smile widened, showing teeth too white to be human. The air around him chilled. "Don't blame me. You trapped them here. I could have sent them on their way back at the stupid beanery. An easy end. But you interfered. You created a romance. An impossible romance. Now they're caught between your light and my mercy. Tell me, which one of us is crueler?"

Perniel said nothing. His silence was grief.

Apollyon leaned close. "Go on then. Tell them they can find their daughter. Tell them there's still hope. Let's see if they believe you."

Perniel turned to Tim and Laura, desperation softening his tone. "You've seen what's possible. You've lived the glimpses. Don't stop now. Choose to go on. Please finish this ride. Keep moving. Maybe you'll find her again. I'll help..."

Apollyon's smile dropped. "Enough." His voice vibrated through the walls. He turned to Laura, his gaze sharp and cold. "It's your choice," he said. "Do you want to keep wandering through pain - or are you ready to be done?"

He looked at Perniel. "Fair? I've given her the choice. It's hers to make. Her 'step to take' if you will."

Perniel shook his head slowly, then gave a reluctant nod. "Fair," he whispered. He looked at Laura with pleading eyes.

Tim turned to his wife. "Laura," he pleaded. "Please. Don't do this. Don't give up. Remember Rose? Her curls, her laugh, the way she'd shout for us from the water? She's waiting. She's out there, somewhere. We can find her. Perniel will help us."

Laura didn't move. Didn't even blink.

Tears cut tracks down her cheeks, but her eyes, those eyes that once burned with love, were dull, hollowed out by exhaustion. She turned back and looked up at Apollyon.

"I'm ready," she said quietly.

"No," Tim whispered, shaking his head with fright. "No, Laura..."

Apollyon smiled, small and satisfied. He turned to Perniel. And flicked his wrist.

Light burst for a moment. Then... nothing. The seat beside Tim was empty.

The sound of the train grew louder and swallowed his scream.

Apollyon turned, his coat gleaming in the flickering light. "See, Perniel? Even love gives up eventually. The prescription... runs out."

Tim rose to his feet, voice shaking but hard. He pointed at Apollyon. "Don't even look at me, you son of a bitch. I'm staying."

Apollyon raised an eyebrow. "Such strong words. Are you sure? You could end this, you know. Go where she went. Let it all fade."

Tim's answer was a growl. "I'm not done. I will find her. I'll bring her back - whatever it takes. I am her warrior. Both of them. I am their warrior."

Apollyon's smirk returned, faint but knowing. "So charming and heroic." He shrugged. "But that's your choice. I got your wife, and..." His eyes glowed red at Tim. "Well, just try and find her." He began to fade, his outline dissolving into the dark like smoke. "Just remember, Perniel," his voice echoed as he vanished. "Love doesn't last forever."

When the last trace of white disappeared, silence returned.

Tim stood there, trembling. The air was thick, electric. The train swayed, and the other souls bowed their heads, their faces dim shapes in the half-light.

Perniel turned toward him. There was something new in the angel's face now, something human. A single tear cut down his cheek. He didn't try to hide it.

Tim's voice broke the silence. "You'll help me find her, won't you?"

Perniel nodded once. "To the end," he said softly.

And for the first time since the beginning of the journey, the train began to slow - not with the sound of brakes, but with the long, mournful sigh of something ancient preparing to stop.

CHAPTER 15

D^{escent}

The train rolled on through perfect darkness. No flicker of light. No sound beyond the dull, eternal hum of motion.

Tim sat rigid, every nerve coiled tight. He was frozen with fear, with the lack of conversation from Laura, memories of Rose on the beach, and with the whole situation. The entire train ride, from the moment he stepped in front of the train to now, moved through his mind and dragged him down deeper into darkness. Across from him, Perniel was still as stone, his hands resting on his knees, his eyes fixed on something only he could see.

For what felt like hours, neither one of them spoke. Then, at last, Tim's whisper broke the silence. "Where do we start?"

Perniel didn't move. His gaze stayed locked ahead, his face unreadable. "I told you I'd help you," he said finally, his voice low, heavy. "But you need to understand, what you're asking is not simple. It isn't safe. It isn't even meant to be possible."

"I don't care how dangerous it is," Tim snapped, grateful that Perniel might not be able to see him and the shape he was in. "I need to find my wife. This..." he gestured around at the endless dark "... was supposed to be our meant-to-be. I have to bring her back." His voice rang through the hollow car, sharp and defiant, echoing back like a challenge hurled at God Himself.

Perniel blinked slowly, his expression softening, but there was sorrow in it too. "I understand," he said. "But—"

"No 'but,'" Tim cut him off, his hands gripping the edge of his seat. He screamed, "You said you'd help! So help!"

For the briefest moment, something like pride flickered across Perniel's face, shimmering with a soft, gold glow. The moment was at hand. He had pushed far enough. Tim was ready. He turned back toward the dark window. "Hold on tight," he said.

Tim frowned. "For what..."

The words never finished.

The train dropped.

No warning. No tilt. Just *gone* - as though the tracks had vanished beneath them.

Tim's body slammed backward into his seat. Air was punched from his lungs. His hands shot out, clawing at the armrests, at the seat, at anything that felt real. His face pulled tight, tears springing from sheer force. Gravity tore at him, dragging his soul downward.

Every instinct screamed - cry out! Beg! Run! But his body wouldn't move. He wasn't sure what he had been expecting, but it wasn't this.

Beside him, Perniel sat motionless. Eyes open. Calm. As if this was exactly what he expected.

Light burst through the train - not from lamps, but from *souls*. They flared like ghostly fireflies, flickering in and out of the car. Some appeared seated beside him for an instant, their forms translucent and trembling, others drifted through the walls as if the train itself were bleeding between worlds.

Men. Women. Children. Young and old. Each one twisted by pain. Their faces contorted. Their mouths opened in soundless agony. And then the silence cracked.

A single scream. Then another. Then hundreds.

It became a *chorus* - a layered, echoing roar that filled every inch of air, clawing at the walls, at Tim's mind, until he thought it would split him open.

Not words. Not cries for help. Just the raw, unfiltered suffering of those condemned to this place.

He wanted to cover his ears, to block it out, but his arms were heavy as iron. His fingers dug into the vinyl seat, white-knuckled.

The train kept falling.

"Are we..." he gasped between shuddering breaths "...are we going to hell?"

No answer.

He turned toward Perniel, his movement slowed by the gravitational forces that held him. The angel's eyes were open but distant, pupils burning faintly with gold light. He was still, unblinking, as if anchored to something outside time.

The walls began to breathe.

Metal swelled and contracted with each pulse, groaning under invisible pressure. Rivets screamed. Sparks flared as the car twisted, rattling so violently it seemed ready to tear in half.

And then the screaming shifted and warped.

It became laughter.

Mocking. Cruel. High-pitched at first, then guttural, like the sound of something imitating joy.

Tim shut his eyes. "Stop! Please! Just stop!"

And then – suddenly - it did.

The fall slowed.
The vibration faded.
The laughter thinned into whispers.
The train leveled.

Tim slumped in his seat, lungs burning, his skin cold and damp. His body still trembled with the echo of motion that wasn't there.

For the first time, he realized the hum beneath them was no longer mechanical - it was alive. The train itself was breathing.

The car crawled forward. Metal against nothing.

Then it stopped.

No hiss of brakes. No station chime. Just stillness.

Tim waited - for light, for the door, for anything. Nothing came. The dark on the other side of the glass was thicker than shadow.

A sound broke it - a creak, slow and drawn out. The door eased open, but no light spilled through. Only *deeper* black.

Perniel rose. His face was pale in the dark, and the gold in his eyes dimmed. "Shall we?" he asked quietly.

Tim swallowed. His throat was dry. "Is this where she is?"

Perniel didn't answer.

He simply extended a hand.

Tim hesitated - then took it. His fingers met warmth, a pulse faint but steady.

"Let's begin," Perniel said.

He stepped through the door and into the void.

Tim followed.

The doors slid shut behind them with a final, echoing *thud*.

CHAPTER 16

The Rescue

When Tim stepped off the train, the first thing he felt was *cold*. Not the cold of weather, but of absence - an emptiness that gnawed through his clothes, through his skin, straight to the bone.

He wrapped his arms around himself, but it did nothing. The air itself rejected warmth.

Perniel stepped off behind him, his face solemn, carved from sorrow. In this place, even the angel's light was dimmed and dulled by the weight of what surrounded them.

"Where are we?" Tim asked, his breath a pale mist.

Perniel didn't answer. He only gestured forward with one slow hand, and the motion carried a command deeper than words.

Tim obeyed.

Each step sank into darkness, the ground soft but endless, as though he were walking on ash. The farther he went, the more he felt it - eyes. Millions of them, unseen but *there*, watching from the black.

Fear rose first. Then horror. Then guilt.

It hit like a tidal wave - *his* guilt. His mistakes, his failures, his regrets pressed in until he could hardly breathe. He wanted to crawl inside himself and die.

After a while, the silence broke. Voices emerged. At first faint, then growing louder, sharper. Screams. Not human cries, but raw anguish torn from countless, condemned throats.

He stopped. The air vibrated with pain. "Is this..." his voice faltered, "...hell?"

Perniel turned slightly, his eyes shadowed, and did not answer. He didn't need to. The silence was enough. Tim knew. Instinctively, he knew.

The darkness thickened as they went. The air grew heavier, pressing against Tim's chest until each breath came shallow and ragged. His heartbeat echoed in his ears like a drum of panic. He wanted to curl into a ball and fall to the ground, praying it all away, but he knew that wasn't an option.

Shapes took form in the black. Trees - crooked, skeletal things that reached upward without branches or leaves. Their bark was dark as pitch. And from each one... hung bodies.

Tim froze.

They weren't simply hanging - they were *part* of the trees, grafted into the wood as though the forest had swallowed them whole. From their arms, their legs, their sides, small, gray creatures crawled and bit, tearing flesh but never killing. Each cry from their lips renewed their torment.

Tim stumbled forward, covering his mouth. His eyes darted from tree to tree. Every voice was an echo of apology, each confession cut short by pain.

"I'm sorry, Mother..." a woman sobbed from above. A creature tore into her arm; she jerked, screamed, then continued her litany of regret. "I'm sorry, Father... it's just that..." Another bite. Another scream. "...it's just that..."

Tim turned away, tears spilling down his cheeks. Another voice caught him - a man's, hoarse and shaking. "I'm sorry, my love... I couldn't take the pressure. I couldn't take the pressure..."
Each repetition cracked his words like dry wood.

Tim's knees buckled. "These are..." He couldn't finish.

Perniel's eyes softened. "The ones from the train. The suicides," he said quietly.

The word hung like judgment, and Tim looked down, trembling. "I feel it," he said. "Deep in my chest. As if..."
He met Perniel's gaze. "...as if *I'm* supposed to be here. As if there's a tree with *my* name on it."

Perniel nodded once, sorrow dark in his eyes. "Now you know."

Tim's voice cracked. "Know what?"

"Where you would've ended up."

The words struck like a blade. Tim froze, breath shallow. Then his memory flooded - the man in white, Laura's surrender, the flick of that pale wrist.

"Wait," he whispered, horror dawning. "Laura. She's here. Isn't she?"

Perniel didn't answer. His silence said everything.

Tim turned, panic rising. "I have to find her. I *have to.*"

Without waiting for a reply, he ran.

The trees stretched on endlessly, each one a monument to despair. Every scream blurred into another. Children called for parents, lovers for lovers, mothers for sons. The air was alive with agony.

And through it all, the creatures fed - never enough to kill, always enough to sustain the torment.

Tim's breath tore in his throat. His legs burned. Still, he ran, tree to tree, face to anguished face, until he could run no longer. His lungs were filling with the ash from the ground and the heaviness of the place. He collapsed, clutching at the dirt.

"LAURA!" he screamed.

The forest went still. It began to spin, around and around him. Faster and faster, his mind reeling, trying to keep up, until... before him, one tree loomed darker than the rest.

Tim lifted his head - and his heart stopped.

She was there.

Laura.

Her body was bound into the bark, pale and motionless, her eyes open but vacant. Her skin was cold stone.

"Laura..." he whispered, stumbling forward. "Laura, can you hear me?"

No answer.

Then, from the base of the tree, a creature scuttled up the trunk. Its claws dug deep, and it sank its teeth into her leg.

Laura jerked. Her mouth opened. "Tim..." she gasped. "I'm sorry, Tim. I'm sorry, Rose. I'm sorry... Uncle Tyrone, forgive me..."

The words repeated, looping endlessly, trapped in grief.

Tim turned to Perniel, desperate for answers, desperate for reprieve for his wife. "How do I get her off of there?"

"I can't help you here," Perniel said softly. "I only brought you to her. What happens next is between you and her."

Tim faced the tree, voice shaking. He had no idea what to do, but he had to try. He had to fight. "Laura, I love you. Please look at me. Hear me."

He dropped to his knees, eyes to the sky, something he had forgotten how to do after his father had left him... alone. "God... whoever's listening... please. Let me take her from here. Let me bring her back. Please."

Silence.

In despair, he screamed, lunged forward, and slammed both fists into the bark. The tree shuddered. Thorns erupted from the wood, piercing his hands. Blood ran freely, dark against the black bark.

He gasped, but he didn't stop. Without thinking, he pressed his hands to her cold skin, and in that instant, something *shifted*.

Her pain flowed into him. His blood into her.

The black faded to gray. Then to pale.

A vision of Susie Moreno back on the train entered his mind unexpectedly, how he had delivered her from this anguish, and Tim realized that he could do this. And only he.

"Laura..." he whispered, pounding again. Each strike drove thorns deeper into his flesh, but he didn't care. He accepted the pain gladly. He kept going, each blow to the tree an act of prayer - each touch to her skin, a touch of love, of defiance to the man in white.

Her arm twitched. Then moved.

"Tim..." she breathed, crying out in hope.

Her left arm came free from the bark. Then her right.

"Tim?" she whispered, blinking through tears. Realization was returning to her soul. "What are you doing here?"

Tim was sobbing now, exhausted, bleeding, but he didn't stop. It was all he could do to continue, but he continued nonetheless. He pressed his hands to her legs. Her body began to loosen, sliding down the trunk.

"She's coming down!" he shouted with happiness that had no place in the dark, dark forest. "She's coming down!"

Perniel nodded from the shadows, silent, reverent. He had no jurisdiction here.

More thorns sprouted and found their way into him. Tim's body shook with pain. He stepped back, then hurled himself forward, slamming into the tree. The spikes tore through him, forcing a blood-curdling scream.

But it worked.

Laura fell into his arms.

His blood and her tears mingled. Her skin warmed beneath his touch. Her breath returned. Her arms rose, wrapping weakly around him, and the thorns - so many thorns that had pierced him - withered and fell to the ashen ground.

They collapsed together at the foot of the tree - broken, naked, and whole all at once.

Tim buried his face against her neck, whispering her name again and again, until her voice met his.

Above them, Perniel raised his hands toward the unseen light.

And they were gone.

When Tim awoke, the sound of wheels filled his ears. The train. He blinked, light flickering above him. He was lying beside Laura on the floor. Their clothes were clean. Her hand was cold against his face, and Tim knew that even though she was with him, things weren't right.

"Thank you, my love," she said softly. "I'm sorry."

Tim smiled through tears. "There's nothing to be sorry for." He leaned in and kissed her.

The train chugged onward into the dark.

They slept, exhausted.

Hours later, brakes squealed. Light filled the car.

Tim helped Laura to her feet. They exchanged a look, not of fear, but of understanding – and, when the doors opened, they stepped into the hospital together, Tim holding on to the emaciated and exhausted form of his wife.

CHAPTER 17

The End of the Line

The hospital room was quiet except for the steady pulse of the monitor and the soft hiss of the respirator. Its rhythm filled the space - a sound too regular, too calm to belong to the world of the living or the dead.

Laura lay beneath thin white sheets, her skin pale and fragile as paper. Tubes ran from her hands to the machines that whispered beside her. She was older now; the tree had done its damage, no matter how much Tim had managed. Her hair streaked with silver, her frame slight beneath the covers, but when she looked up at Tim, her eyes were the same as they had been the last three days.

She smiled beneath her oxygen mask. "Hello, my love."

Tim leaned in and kissed her forehead. "Hello, my love. How are you feeling today?"

Her breath came slow and shallow. "I feel like... I'm finally there," she whispered. "All the sadness... the depression... the loss... It's all going to be okay now."

She closed her eyes. Tim reached for her hand, folding it gently into his own. A faint warmth pulsed between their palms - not heat, but something softer, almost like memory itself.

Flashes came to them, memories shared...
Rose.
Virginia Beach.
The golden field.
A soccer ball rolling across perfect grass.
Her laughter echoing in sunlight.
The bike rides.
The swimming.
The moments of joy carved into eternity.

Each image flickered through him, bright and fading, like light passing between worlds.

Laura stirred, opening her eyes again. "It's getting closer," she said.

He nodded. "I know, my love. I know."

"They're trying to save me... back there in the real world. Doctors, nurses. I heard them. 'We're losing her.'" Her breath shuddered. "But then... something changed. I think they..." She met his eyes again, tears forming. "Tim, you were the only reason I stayed. You and those ridiculous jokes." She shuddered a laugh, and Tim joined her. He brushed gently at her cheek.

"Well, if that's true, then I'm never stopping," he spoke softly. He brushed at her hair and smiled. His words were tender. "You know, I've been reading a book on gravity. It's impossible to put down."

Laura smiled. "Ugh." She tried to roll her eyes.

Neither of them felt fear anymore. Only peace - the slow settling of the soul before it sleeps. They had made it through the horror of the darkness, the sadness, and now that they had reached the end of the line, they couldn't change the facts placed in front of them. They were too late.

Laura closed her eyes once more, and the current between them deepened. This time, Tim saw more than flashes. He saw the *after*.

The quiet years. The rebuilding. The long mornings that began in silence but ended in laughter. The ordinary days that had somehow become holy.

They never could find Rose again, and the grief devoured them both. Laura had slipped into a darkness Tim couldn't name, but she never stepped onto the train again. Tim - steady, patient, devoted - had remained by her side through it all.

They tried to have another child. They couldn't. Still, he stayed.

Years passed, and they aged together - silver creeping into their hair, wrinkles etching stories into their hands. They took long walks through parks, traveled when they could, and laughed when they were able. And though Laura was never quite the same, Tim loved her still. Always would.

Now, here where they began, somewhere on the train, off the train... somewhere... her breath shallow and her heart slowing, they watched their shared life play backward - a film unraveling to its first frame. They saw what could have been, what never was, what almost was. And they forgave it all.

Tim opened his eyes. The vision faded. Laura's chest rose and fell, a fragile rhythm.

"Maybe," he whispered, always full of optimism, "this isn't the end of the line."

Laura smiled under the mask. "It is for me," she said softly.

He tilted his head. "Maybe not for me. Maybe somewhere on the train... if I ride it long enough... I can find the beginning again, and we can start over."

Laura gave a soft, breathy laugh, ending in a light cough that shook her body. When it passed, she smiled again and closed her eyes. "You always were the hopeful one."

Tim brushed her hair again and stayed quiet, listening to the machines. The rhythm reminded him of another hum - steel wheels against unseen rails.

He could almost feel it again.

The train.

The space between worlds.

The silence between stations.

The pulse of the in-between.

The heart monitor ticked slower now - three beats, two, one...

Tim lifted his gaze toward the hallway.

There stood Perniel.

The conductor. The guardian. The angel who had carried them through so many crossings. He was the same, his blonde hair glowing faintly in the sterile light, his expression unreadable, his eyes filled with both grief and quiet pride.

Tim smiled faintly. "Do you think there's another stop on the line?"

Perniel's lips curved into something close to a smile. He shrugged, palms open, "I don't know. Maybe. That's up to you."

Tim turned back to Laura and took her hand again. Another wave of memory rose between them, but this time, it wasn't his. It was hers.

He saw the girl she once was - small, frightened, passed from home to home. He saw her loneliness. Her first razor. The night she almost didn't make it.

And then - the train.

And then - *him.*

Meeting her on that strange, endless ride between life and death. Choosing love. Choosing each other...

Then the vision faded.

Tim opened his eyes.

The monitor had gone still.

No sound. No pulse. Only the hush of the respirator winding down.

He leaned close. "Laura?" No answer. "Laura..."

Her face was still. Peaceful.

She was gone. They had finally saved her. Back there. Back in the real world.

Tim's hand trembled around hers, but he didn't cry. Not this time. He only looked toward Perniel.

The angel's gaze was soft, waiting.

Tim took a breath. "Let's go try," he said quietly.

He bent down, kissed Laura's forehead, and whispered, "I'll see you in a few minutes."

Then he closed his eyes and was gone.

CHAPTER 18

Final Destination

He was back on the train. Only this time, he rode alone. The dad jokes were gone, save for that final, tender moment with Laura. There had been no reason for them since... well, since Rose had started hurting herself. There was nothing inside of him that wanted to joke around anymore.

The car was empty, washed in dim gray light, the hum of the rails deep and low. The weight of Laura's death pressed against his chest, heavy as stone. Grief thickened the air until every breath felt earned.

He loved her still. Even after all they had endured. After all the years that were days – through all the pain, all the loss, love was the one thing the darkness had never managed to take. The prescription from Dr. Joe had worked, and somewhere deep inside, beyond fear and despair, he held a single fragile hope: that this might work. That their meant-to-be wasn't finished.

The train rumbled through the void.

At the far end of the car stood the man in white, his back turned, hands gliding methodically from soul to soul. Each flick of his wrist sent another presence into the trees beyond the windows - those same black trees that filled the landscape of Tim's nightmares. He tried not to look. Tried not to remember what had hung from their branches.

He turned away, eyes shut tight, forcing the memory back. But memory has its own gravity, and it clung to him like fog.

Still, nothing could shake his resolve.

The train rolled on a little farther, wheels screaming softly as they slowed. Then came the long metallic shriek of brakes - the same sound that always marked an ending.

Followed by... silence.

No light from the windows above. No flickering bulbs. Just stillness.

Tim knew this stop. Knew it in his bones.

A strange feeling came over him as he stood, and he patted the pocket of his jeans. He took out the pill bottle that was there, the one Dr. Joe had given him, and he smiled at the label: Rx – LOVE. TAKE ONE PILL AS NEEDED. Tim shook the bottle, narrowed his eyes, and opened the lid. He poured the contents out into his hand. One pill.

"Just for good measure," he looked at it and then quickly swallowed it dry.

Dropping the bottle to the floor of the train, he took one final look around the car and stepped off.

The moment his feet touched the ground, the air changed. Pressure closed around his throat. He reached up instinctively and froze. His fingers brushed coarse rope.

He was swaying. Back and forth. Toes grazing the floor.

His lungs convulsed. Panic surged like lightning through his body. This was where it began.

His memories roared back as Tim tried to fill his brain with the tiny bit of oxygen that he had tried to eliminate. He hadn't stepped in front of a train after all. That had been the fantasy - his mind's mercy.

This - this was the truth.

He remembered. The ceiling fan in the kitchen. The looped rope. The whisper of despair that had told him it would be easier this way.

It would have been easier to step in front of a train.

But death here was slow. Deliberate.

The rope bit into his neck. His vision darkened at the edges. The world shrank to heartbeat and pain.

He kicked. Hard.

The noose tightened.

Each desperate swing drew blood, stripped skin, tore air from his chest. His body betrayed him, thrashing toward nothing.

Then - *SNAP.*

The fan broke loose and dangled by the electrical wires holding it in place, but somehow the rope uncoiled.

Tim crashed to the floor, gasping.

The world blurred in a haze of pain and disbelief. His back screamed, his throat burned, but he was alive.

He tore the rope from his neck, gulping air like water, and real-ized... he was *home.*

The train was gone. He was standing in his kitchen.

The air was still. The faint scent of coffee lingered. Afternoon light spilled through the window.

On the table: his car keys, and beside them - his note.

He stared at it for a moment. *To whoever finds me...*

Then he crushed it in his fist, shoved it into the trash, and didn't look back.

He grabbed the keys and ran.

Down the steps. Out the door. Into his car.

The engine roared to life. Tires screamed against pavement.

He drove like a man reborn.

Tim didn't stop until the city rose before him.

Streetlights blinked to life. The air was sharp, alive with noise. He skidded into a parking spot, breath ragged, heart pounding.

A horn blared as he swung open the door - he jumped back just in time to avoid being run over, laughter breaking through his panic. He leaned against the car, chest heaving, half-crying, half-laughing at the irony.

Then he saw it.

Across the street - the café.

The same one. He knew he had recognized it. The neon sign glowed soft blue against the dusk.

He stared at the building, hardly daring to believe.

He crossed the street, weaving through traffic, heart hammering. The bell above the café door chimed as he stepped inside.

Warm light. Soft voices. The clink of silverware. The smell of roasted beans and sugar.

Unlike the train, this diner was full. Not with ghosts, but with *people.* Real people.

Tim frantically scanned from table to table, his eyes searching and hoping until... there, in the corner booth...

Laura.

Her hair framed her face in loose curls, and she held a cup of coffee between both hands, the steam curling upward like a prayer.

She looked up.

Their eyes met.

Her smile bloomed, gentle, knowing, whole.

Tim's breath caught. He crossed the floor without realizing his feet were moving.

"Is this seat taken?" he asked, his voice trembling.

Laura's smile widened. She reached for his hand. "Only by you," she said.

He bent and kissed her, and for an instant the world tilted, light and air blending into one long sigh.

He sat across from her, unable to look away. In her eyes, he saw everything - the train, the darkness, the rescue, the love that had carried them through.

They remembered it *all.* They *had* shared it all.

Quietly, he asked the only question that mattered.

"Are you ready?"

Laura nodded. "I am."

"Are you sure?"

"As sure as I've ever been."

He smiled. "Then let's go get our meant-to-be."

They stood, hands entwined, and walked toward the door.

Just before stepping outside, Laura stopped. She looked up at him, eyes bright, lips curved in a teasing grin.

"We're not taking the train, are we?"

Tim laughed, shaking his head. "No. I have my car."

She grinned back. "Good."

He paused, glancing toward the twilight beyond the glass. "But somewhere down the road," he said softly, "we're going to need a van."

Laura's smile deepened. "I hope so."

Hand in hand, they stepped out into the evening.

The door swung shut behind them, the bell chiming once, like the echo of a distant whistle fading into the light.

They walked on, together, ready for their meant-to-be.

EPILOGUE

The Golden Field

The field stretched wide beneath a slow-turning sun, gold light spilling across the grass until every blade shimmered like memory. The wind carried the hum of summer - cut grass, salt from the nearby shore, and the sound of children shouting across the distance.

Tim and Laura sat on an old wooden bench near the edge of the field. The world felt still, too still, as if waiting to see if they'd notice how alive it was.

Laura's hand rested on her stomach, a faint curve beneath her light dress. Tim's fingers folded gently over hers. Neither spoke for a while. There was no need. The air around them was thick with the kind of quiet that comes only after storms.

Finally, Laura broke the silence. "It's strange," she said softly, her eyes following the motion of a ball arcing through the sunlight. "After everything we've been through... this feels ordinary. Almost peaceful."

Tim smiled faintly. "Maybe that's the miracle," he said.

She turned toward him, sunlight catching in her hair. "You think this is real?"

He hesitated. "I keep waiting to wake up on that train again. But this..." He looked out across the field, the laughter, the trees swaying at the edges of the light. "This feels solid. Like something we've earned."

Laura's eyes softened. "Do you think we'll do better this time? If this really is... another beginning?"

Tim squeezed her hand. "We already are. You're here. I'm here. The baby's here. And that's enough for now."

She smiled and brushed his knuckles with her thumb. "I still feel her with us, you know? Like she never really left. Like she's still one foot there and one foot here. I don't know, maybe that's what second chances are for, to carry love forward, even when it changes shape."

He nodded. "Then maybe we're finally ready."

For a moment, nothing moved but the light. A whistle cut across the air, sharp, distant, and then a chorus of cheers erupted from the field.

Laura turned toward the sound. At first, it was just another youth game, bright jerseys, flying hair, parents clapping from the sidelines. But then a single voice carried through the din:

"Go, Rose!"

Laura froze. Her breath caught in her throat.

Tim shaded his eyes, scanning the field. A girl was running down the line, chasing the ball. The same quick stride, the same blonde curls tumbling in the sun.

He couldn't speak.

Laura stood slowly, tears already streaking her face. "Tim..."

He stood beside her, both of them rooted for one impossible heartbeat. Then, together, they began to walk. Hesitant steps at first - fear, disbelief, wonder all tangled together. The laughter grew louder. The cheers swelled.

When the girl turned - just enough for the sunlight to catch her face - they broke.

Tim and Laura started to run.

Down the hill, through the tall grass, toward the sound of life calling them home.

At the far edge of the field, a horse stamped in the glow of the fading light, its mane rippling like gold thread. Nearby, a tall, blonde figure watched - quiet, peaceful, hands folded before him. For a moment, the air shimmered around his shoulders, a hint of white fire. Then he was gone, leaving only the whisper of wind through the reeds.

Tim and Laura never saw him. They were already at the field, laughter and tears indistinguishable, the world spilling open before them.

The ball rolled to a stop near their feet. Footsteps followed until... ten-year-old Rose looked at them and smiled, a smile that nearly broke both of their hearts. "You found me." Her voice sang in their ears like the voices of a thousand angels.

Tim, sobbing in between the laughter, wrapped his arms around her. "Rose... we'd cross every universe to find you. Even the ones where my jokes are worse."

Rose tilted her head and smiled - a smile that crossed galaxies. "Daddy, your jokes are always bad."

Laura laughed, a laugh full of release from everything that had been haunting her for so long. "And yet... we still love you, Tim."

Laura stepped into the hug, and for the first time in forever, everything was right.

THE END

...Somewhere, in a world not yet seen, a whistle sounded again. None of them heard it. Not yet.

Will Phillips Hallewell has been writing for many years across a wide range of genres - from spiritual reflections to teen sports fiction. His stories often draw from the threads of his own life. Take One Step holds a particularly special place in his heart, reflecting experiences and emotions that have shaped him over the years.